DAWNS OF EXORDIUM

HeartString Publishing
a Division of Stone Creek Farms
P.O. Box 734
Airway Heights, WA 99022

First Edition: October 2019
Printed in the United States of America
ISBN: 13: 978-1-7321401-3-4

PREFACE AND ACKNOWLEDGMENTS

Exordium: Latin meaning "beginning" or "from the start." Hence our title implies, dawns from the beginning. Our small group of writers found that a couple of stories shared a common theme of new beginnings. From that recognition we determined we should each write a "creation story."

It was fun to see what the prompt inspired and we hope our readers will enjoy each offering as much as we did.

We wish to acknowledge May Cotton and Roseanne Lasater for being the "founding mothers" of our writing group. *Not Your Mother's Writing Group* came into being out of a frustration of being silenced for uncomfortable subjects and word usage. Though very diverse in thought, politics, religion, and temperament, each member has felt welcomed and free to voice their thoughts through their writing without fear of censorship. The nurturing environment provided by our pseudo mother has allowed each writer to dare to share and move forward with our chosen forms of self-expression.

Speaking of mothers, the use of the tree of life motif was a deliberate choice. In Hebraic tradition, Wisdom was a woman represented by a tree. It was understood that she was the wife of Yahweh and that all creation came through her. Many of us have read of her and know her by the name Asherah. Her mystique and the myths about her were corrupted. Speaking of wisdom, in the book of Proverbs one can read that the world was made through wisdom.

> She is a tree of life to them that lay hold upon her:
> and happy is every one that retaineth her.
>
> — Proverbs 3:18 KJV

For this reason it should not surprise the reader to find women creators among the stories collected for this anthology. Again, we wish to acknowledge that without each member of our writing group, this book would never have come to be. A state of being, a beginning, exordium.

CONTENTS

The world didn't look any different to her. Through her window, Cora saw the same blue skies, the same powdery snow. They had all four seasons, which Daddy loved, and the sun did its usual rising in the East. Though all of that would change.

Three witches had taken her world. They'd carried it to the dark cave where the caldron boiled and caged locusts refused to sing. The witches had brought Cora's world in the form of a bubble, a delicate impenetrable bubble in which it floated, bringing it through the rocky tunnel straight to the caldron, covered in cobwebs for the passage. It was now held over the boiling liquid by hands so old as to be skeletal.

She still lived in her world, mind you, Cora did, and so did everyone she knew. She lived there with her older sister, her mama and daddy, and they'd been very happy in their oasis out in the country. Her parents had built a humble cottage, surrounding it with a vast yard, edging it with gardens and sheds. Brightly colored fields with wind-swept grasses extended beyond sight, channeling breezes that scattered dandelion seeds and blew tumbleweeds across the fields. They flowed down the hill—the fields, the breeze, the tumbleweeds—on which the family lived, toward the little dirt road below that took them to the city.

But things were about to change. The witches would be sure of that. Cora's world would continue like always, everything looking just as it had been the day before. But things would not really be as they were—not even close. Cora wouldn't notice the difference at first, because the stars, the sun, all the atmosphere and everything below would look the same, even though they'd been shoved in a bubble that now hovered above a witch's caldron.

***

"We've got it," said one of the sisters in a high pitch voice that sounded like she'd swallowed sandpaper moments prior. The other two witches giggled till she shrieked, causing the one holding the globe to almost drop it. That silenced them all.

"We've been cut off," said the second witch, in a low willowing voice. Her name was Izzy, her sisters: Totem and Lore. "She'll pay for it."

"We'll cut her off just as surely as we were," said Lore, "and she'll live in this cave with us."

"A listening slave," Totem popped, looking very pleased with herself, "A prisoner who has to listen to everything we say."

Lore tipped back, sucking in air helplessly, and then doubled over to release it. She laughed so hard the veins in her neck bulged and she turned red in the face.

Izzy remained focused, squinting her eyes till only the glint of one remained, flickering with the twitching of an eyelid and staring straight ahead. "We will go for the mother first." She cast her spell.

"The mother," Lore repeated in a singing way that sounded sweet and dowdy, but also slithering and shrill.

"The mother . . ." Totem whispered.

All three sisters chanted, rhythmically, peering into Cora's small world. The bubble hardened but fragile still, hung from a chain, and dangled, just above the boiling line of their giant pot. "Take the mother," they said, rolling eyes back in their heads.

***

Cora lay on her full-sized bed. The quilt reminded her of Mama who made the sheets so smooth and draped the corners just so. Mama always made the house smell clean and soapy, and she sewed clothes for them to wear to school and church. Cora's mama had always been so strong and clever, not at all like Daddy, a delicate and sensitive soul. Cora had been the delight of Mama, though a pain to her sister, who was Daddy's favorite—though Daddy would always be Daddy to Cora. Sister was kind enough if Cora let her have her way, and her mama was always there to talk to.

Some woman came tapping on the front door, an oddly beautiful woman. She'd come to talk to Mama, to complain that Cora and her sister were not keeping up at school. They did not organize as they should, the woman said, and they never cleaned after themselves—which wasn't true. Cora was never in trouble at school and her sister only struggled with her reading. But Mama didn't argue; she only looked dazed and somehow distant. She didn't even ask who the woman was, nor did she defend either child, not even a little.

This woman had driven a long way on those dusty roads

for this, which was strange to Cora, and the way Mama responded to her made Cora wonder if they'd met before. Cora's sister eavesdropped from the hallway, and Cora stood right behind her.

Mama pleaded with the woman desperately.

"It's you," said the beauty, going through their cupboards one at a time. "You're their mama. You're to blame for all their bad behavior."

"It's their daddy!"Mama cried, stunning the girls, as did her standing there wringing her hands. "Their daddy spoils the children, no matter how hard I try, and he won't stop, no matter what I say. It's all his fault!" Cora's mama cried, "Blame him, not me!"

"It's you," the woman said before departing. She was unyielding and shook her beautiful face, now harsh and unforgiving. She had no time for Mama's excuses. The woman seemed gravely disappointed when she left, like someone who belonged to their family once, an aunt or a grandma, but no one Cora ever met.

***

"The sister," Izzy said. All three witches were now swaying slightly from side to side from the waist up. The caldron boiled before them and the bubble just hung there, still covered in spider webs. The witches no longer strained to keep their eyes rolled back. It was as if the pupils could no longer be found. They'd been glued or hitched to something on the top of their brain, some hook maybe, hidden just under the skull. Captivated by the work of their enchantment, the witches hummed nasally. "The sister," they all muttered through unmoving lips. "Take the sister . . ."

***

Sister came running out of the hallway the moment the strange woman left, and she began screaming the most beastly things at their mama. She said things no little girl should ever say, swearing and spitting and exploding into small tantrums. Cora tried to reason with her older sister; this wasn't Mama's fault. It was a strange accusing woman, and Mama wasn't herself. Cora's sister swatted at her so violently and with such reach Cora stepped back in fear. Sister kept up her demands that changed as she went on raging at their mama. Sister had stopped defending Daddy, and she began to order Mama to open her purse. Mama would give Sister money for candy, Sister said, or Sister would scream all day.

Cora held her head in her hands. The beginning of a headache was throbbing in her little temples. A woman had come to the house and Mama had blamed Daddy for bad behavior that neither Cora nor her sister were guilty of, and she couldn't make sense of it. As Sister grew more demanding and shrill, Cora thought she might scream, but her sister kept shouting and Mama kept running about the house giving Sister whatever she wanted, which was never enough. Under her breath and between Sister's huffs and puffs, Cora thought she heard her mama say, "Wait till your daddy gets home."

Soon Sister turned on Cora, making her scrape up whatever money she had in her room, bits of candy too, if she had it. Sister told Cora that her little sister owed her "penance," for all Cora had ever done wrong, including her birth. Sister then sent Mama on an errand saying, "I'll search your room myself." She then marched off, and while Cora worried about what her sister might feel entitled to, she dared not stop her.

***

"The daddy," Totem began the chant, but the witch, Izzy, stopped her.

"Let the mother finish him off and the sister, too," Izzy said. "Cora has a soft spot in her heart for him, so let him lose his mind as he loses his family, the same as she."

Totem protested, "But the daddy's to be a wolf, remember? To hunt Cora down in the yard before he rips her to shreds. I've planned for months to use this spell."

"'Tis true, Izzy," Lore backed Totem, hocking up a small frog from her throat and biting it once before tossing it into the boiling brew.

"'Tis unimportant," Izzy waved her hand dismissively. "The daddy stays as he is. Perhaps he will try to save Cora. It is always better to get their hopes up before dashing them to pieces."

"He stays as he is," Lore agreed obediently, knowing the importance of voting. With three sister-witches there was always an odd-girl-out; three was a terrible number. Totem said nothing. She only cracked her one knuckle, her lipless frown remained stiff.

***

It was almost dark and the moon had already floated up along that invisible string that pulled it into the sky. The shouting continued. Her daddy came home to Cora's mama begging her sister to just be comforted, content with what she'd already taken, which was everything. Mama turned on Daddy, like a cat baring its fangs, and after Daddy realized this was what he was in for, for the rest of the evening, he began to shout back. Daddy was stunned by Cora's sister as well, and told her to return all of Cora's clothing, since Cora's closet was now bare from her sister's plucking, as was her underwear drawer, emptied of her softest nightgowns. One might have thought Daddy had asked Sister to part from a dear pet, a kitten she'd nursed back from the threshold of a premature death, the way Sister fought his request. And Daddy couldn't win, because whenever Sister was silent, preoccupied for a moment, Mama nagged, blaming him for spoiling the girls and insisting he do something now, now, now, to discipline them.

Cora did stop to cry then, no longer able to withstand the molten anger between her parents. She'd never seen them fight, and all she wanted was what she'd always had, the whole beautiful family getting along. *But had it really been that way before?* It was like a voice on her shoulder. *Did her family really ever like each other? How long had this been happening?* The voice asked. *All this blaming and shaming, and little girls swearing.*

Daddy shouted like a helpless beast surrounded by jackals, Sister's demands and Mama's new rules. Cora somehow managed to get her sister to take a nap, realizing that all the tantrums were taking a toll on her. But just as soon as Sister fell asleep, when Cora could feel her sister's beating heart slowing, her sister woke with a start by their mama, who burst through the bedroom door, shouting about trolls and piles of clothes. Surprisingly, Cora's sister only rolled out of bed. Her little feet carried her to the kitchen and she flung open the pantry, tearing open a package of cake mix she poured fistfuls of sugary powder down her throat.

This wasn't Cora's gentle family, she thought. Her daddy wasn't to blame. Their mama didn't yell. Cora and her sister always had chores and always earned good marks at school. Now, Mama forced Cora to clean her room, only insisting she slave, fold everything perfectly, sort it just so in the closets, whatever Sister had left her. Mama even wanted the shirts hung in order and two fingers apart, something only Daddy ever did.

Daddy was going crazy, and he started to pace nervously. Mama told him to fashion a whip to stripe the girls, and Cora finally got angry at that. It was her first moment of outrage, and Cora might have whispered something to her sister, but Sister was shoving buttery popcorn into her mouth from a bucket she used to hold far more than she could eat. In between mouthfuls, Sister reported to Mama that she would not be returning to school from then on. She said it matter-of-factly as she went to rifle through Mama's fine jewelry. To Cora's surprise Mama said nothing, just excoriated Daddy for spoiling the children, and Cora began to believe that when their mama said "children" she only meant Cora.

Cora's daddy could have defended himself against Mama's new cleaning demands—Daddy had always been tidier than Mama anyway—but he couldn't abide by whipping of children, and that had Cora running into Daddy's arms. He picked her up and she could still feel their heart connection. That's what the family called the warm and happy feelings they had together, especially when they played games, used ice skates and rode ponies. But Mama and Sister were impossible to reach, the heart connection Cora had with them had been severed, or so it seemed, but not Daddy. Daddy was still there.

Cora was beginning to believe her life before had been a dream, that somehow things had always been this way. Not the family she thought she knew, but the one storming her home, had been there all along. She must have been asleep and forgotten somehow, in some kind of trance, when she imagined herself laying peacefully on Mama's smoothed out bed linens, or cleaning the house with a song on her lips, leaving the scent of flowers and soap. No, Cora decided, she'd never sat at her mama's feet while she sewed clothing, because, like her mama said, she only ever wanted them in the best silks, the finest buttons. Home-sewn clothes would never do.

Mama's obsessions had shifted as violently as Sister's demands. Mama wanted piles of gold now, but Daddy wasn't a goldminer. He wasn't even rich. At least he lacked the wealth for what Cora's mama had planned, a fine white dress with golden lace and jeweled shoes for each girl; they were meant to help the children improve at school. She also wanted tutors for each, and nannies, and servants, and a moat around their home. Daddy resisted, because they couldn't afford it. Mama persisted, he would have to abandon his job and go to medical school, even though he was an accountant. Mama insisted on a bigger house, too. The bigger the house, she'd said, the whiter the front picket fence, the better the girls would behave—with regular whippings. But in the solace of Daddy's arms, Cora realized all was lost. He put her back down on the floor and released her from the warm hug, and this washed-over look darkened his face. "You are just like your mother," he said, "always wanting something," and Cora knew she'd lost him. Daddy no longer had the joy in his eyes, the kind he always had when he looked at Mama. She remembered how his looking at her always made him happy for their likeness, but now Daddy seemed to hate Cora. Cora thought she'd heard a low dangerous growl rise from her daddy's throat, and she stepped back, tripping when she saw his eyeteeth and imagined fangs. His eyes turned black like a wolf's, before he finally burped, looking quite surprised by the force of it.

Then something happened. She saw a trace of his love again. All his love for her, for their mama, came flooding back into his momentarily pale face. He hugged Cora tenderly again. Holding her at arm's length, he said, "Something is wrong with us. There's something wrong with your mama."

"Sister too," Cora whispered, trusting him for all the world.

Rage flashed in his face again. "Don't you dare hurt your sister," he growled. Then he let out a shout that drove her back and down to the floor, right in his long shadow that stretched over and past her. His pupils and the irises turned pitch black so you could not tell one from the other.

***

"The daddy," Lore danced around. "The daddy, too. Let's see how long Cora survives with him under our spell."

"Did you slip in the wolf spell?" Izzy asked Totem with suspicious squinty eyes.

"He should be a wolf!" Totem snarled. Izzy came scurrying over so fast that her pointy shoes squeaked on the floor. She'd lifted her tattered skirt, exposing long, vertically striped socks before puffing up to her sister. Totem hissed and did the same, the two of them looked like balding birds posturing to fight. Lore had to break them up, reminding them of all the grisly things they meant to do.

Izzy placed her spindly hands, boney fingers sprawled, over the boiling caldron. She felt the heat of it warm her palms. "Come out," she ordered her sister's spell, and tiny liquid orbs of wolf-powder lifted from the putrid stew.

"Do not!" Totem danced around, much stealthier and nimble for her age, the cobwebs matching the grey of greasy hair tangled like a rat's nest about her shoulders. She howled like a low-flying vulture, clipped by a car and run under the tires, when Izzy pulled all of the wolf-powder she could out of the pot and threw it against the wall of the cave. Totem's howling turned to shrieking, the kind that pierced the echoing cave when she laughed, now her chuckles were only painful spasms that rose from a pile of witch on the floor.

"This is best," Izzy said, continuing the conversation with Lore as if their sister, Totem, wasn't laying there fetal-like by the base of the caldron.

"Did you see that moment," Lore said to Izzy, indifferent to Totem, "just before we zapped him?"

"Oh, yes," Izzy assured her. "That precious moment of *fatherly affection*," she said with sneering contempt.

"You know what that means." Lore pointed to Izzy. "She'll get stronger. We never should have let him go so long."

"She was only strong for a fleeting moment," Izzy declared. "Hush now. It's why we took him. Cora will die," she insisted, as Totem heaved out her last angry breath.

"Cora will die." Totem rose, rejoining the others, nodding obediently, eagerly, as if she'd never forgotten it.

"Cora dies," Lore finished the circle, and they all took their places. "First, we throw her into despair."

***

But Cora didn't die, for a white fox came calling at the entrance of the witch's cave. He was a wizard, and like the others, he never trimmed his mustache and salted beard, or cut a hair on his head, letting it flow long and grey over his shoulders. A master of his craft, the fox usually abided in a vast workshop, toiling in the Great Forest where he tumbled and forged the landscapes of his worlds. Day after day, donning his white apron, he formed the mountains and caverns for above and below the waters that he sprinkled on seeded land. Before lunch, he blew glassy clouds, sanded white stone into snow, and on Wednesdays he weathered his worlds to perfection.

The best way to travel the Crooked Wood, the realm of the three witches, was on paw, with pallid frost drifting from a fluffy tail. He bounded through the forest because, as a fox, he needed no hands or tools for his task. He wasn't there to craft a world but to retrieve one, the one that now hung above a witch's caldron. His magic would let no one die, not from mischief anyway, and even his fur, shed and carried on the wind, quieted the dark woodland magic—for the time being.

Cora's world could have used more weathering, the heat of his forge or the glacial baths in his utility sink. It was too young for what he'd tried to do, putting it in to a bubble, a shell to withstand the frozen cold of the mountain passes. On his way, the witches stole it from the gap in the mountainous rock where he'd put it, to free up his hands momentarily. He'd fought with a loose peg in his silver buckle when they'd snatched it, and he'd been trying to cinch his great fur coat because the wind kept flinging it open.

The fox had been taking the world over the mountain in the middle of winter, unfinished; it was his final attempt to save face. The others had scolded him nonstop for growing attached, making it his pastime and habit to take the world home, let it blaze on his night table and soothe him to sleep. The passes were kindlier in the spring, lined in plunging waterfalls, curvy brooks and sweet wildflowers, but he meant to avoid the big festival, where wizards gathered to caravan. They'd sing in low tones and perfect harmony as they traveled with heaving bags and wobbly carts filled with their creations. All were to be sold at a vast Market on the other side.

The fox tried to take Cora's world early, secretly, since they'd caught him gazing dreamily at the little family—the father, mother and precious girls. They still had no idea he'd cheated the witches, for when it was his turn to distribute the magical rations for the year, he siphoned just enough of the witches share to make Cora's eyes bright as a green star. He'd hoped the witches wouldn't notice.

But Magic was to be divided up between the Great Forest and the Crooked Wood evenly, and worlds were not playthings for bored wizards at night. When he heard of the witches plot to kill the girl, he'd come to make things right, knowing he never should have taken it out of the shop, let alone brave the mountain pass alone.

He stole into the cave, listening. His silvery fur gleamed in the darkness, as he made it to the opening in the back where the black, stinking caldron bubbled. The witches stood, their bottles of pickled rot and half-eaten jars of thumbs and eyeballs on a shelf behind them. Planks were affixed to the cave wall with barnacle glue from the sea, holding their jars next to caged broken-winged bats and a colony of maggots on a severed arm swinging on a meat hook.

The wizard had to be clever, especially after he heard about the wolf powder Totem dumped in the caldron. The fox listened carefully when Totem and Izzy had bickered about it. He'd heard Totem's fake tantrum, after her sister Izzy drew the wolf powder back out of the hellish stew, throwing it against the cave wall. Izzy was kidding herself if she thought wolf powder could be removed that easily, he thought, especially when the likes of a witch like Totem had mixed it.

Totem's protests were too thunderous to be real, and the fox knew it was a distraction. She wanted her sisters to be cruel as she howled and cried, turning their gaze away as she slipped more powder into the foul-smelling mix. The fox peeked around the corner just in time to see her looking knowingly over her shoulder at the other two, who sweetly spoke to each other, colluding to reject her. When Izzy and Lore allowed Totem back into their little circle, Totem grinned into the pot triumphantly. Totem loved her evil hounds, the three-headed dogs and werewolves, and she refused to reap death and destruction if one of the species were not involved in the plot.

But Izzy caught a glance of the satisfaction in Totem's eyes, the older sister's attention became sharp as an elven blade. Her bloodshot eyes flashed up at the glittering wolf powder that she'd thrown against the cave wall, glowing like monster snot, and then at Totem's hand covered in it. Totem doubled down on the howling, crying louder and more pathetically than before, but Izzy saw through it and she licked her mouth with a slimy tongue.

Totem's eyes shifted nervously back and forth. Izzy dropped her spoon and cornered her. Lore prepared to punish their mischievous sister in any grizzly way Izzy decided. Totem had gone against the coven, against the circle, and they would make her pay for it.

"I am the eldest sister!" Izzy sneered. "I said no wolf!" She wagged her finger, then stopped for a long, hair-raising pause. Izzy's eyes were so wide the fox saw all the whites, or the yellows, all around them, and she froze, stabbing Totem with a fixed glare. Finally, Totem grew incensed, standing erect and squaring off, she stood as tall as a bent hag could stand, her gaze proud as a woodland stag, her expression venomous as a yellow-lipped snake. She faced Izzy and they started hopping again, circling like cocks in a fight. Frightened, Lore stretched between her sisters, spread-eagle, with hands clutching each of them by their grey dresses.

It wasn't just that the sister-witches were loud, they were engrossed in their blood-chilling conflict. And a witch's ear heard every little thing—a feather landing or footsteps in the sand by a roaring ocean—but, for now, their fury drowned out the sound of the fox padding to the caldron. *Brilliant witches,* he thought. One could always count on them eating their own–at least till their rivalry succumbed to their hive mind, the collective thoughts of the coven, a sacred sisterhood that should never be underestimated. The fox shrunk down to crawl like a beetle, to the thick jagged edge of the pot. Then he flew the span of inches onto Cora's world, letting himself fall into the sky.

***

He landed gently on human feet, feeling the long hair on his shoulders, and the hem of his robe brushing his ankles. He was where he wished to be, on the land of Cora's parents, where they'd carved out a charming life that took on a life of its own. As the fox hurried to the cottage, he took in the countryside that he'd forged. With his own hands, he shaped it, adding all the little features of his best handiwork. Feeling the smooth and cooling dust ground in his tumbler, the clean, brown dirt between his toes, he tasted the moisture of cold pockets that he'd poured and frozen, melted and evaporated, till they burst into clouds and rained, over and over again. It was a repeating cycle that was hard to get right, but impossible to stop once it started.

Cora's spine-tingling scream and the guttural sounds of her daddy's growl propelled the fox out of his wistfulness. The sun had fallen, and the world was beyond dim, the moon sparkled in pieces, shadowed in clouds that would soon clear. The fox shifted to four legs and arrived just in time to see Cora's daddy change, towering over shreds of his own clothing and bristling with fur all over his body. Not one inch of his skin wasn't covered, and he was glorious and muscular, a perfect wolf. His black form reflected the blue hues in the moonlight that now flooded from the white circle in the sky, and his big, glossy fangs dripped with wolf slobber.

Cora sprawled on her back before the beast, lifting herself up on hands and feet, she began pulling herself away, like a crab, scrambling till she could spin around and run for her life. Her daddy was somewhere in the center of a hungry wolf, inhaled into its core. He'd succumbed to bizarre hunger, an inexplicable hatred for prey that he no longer recognized as his daughter.

But the fox understood. He had his own canine impulses to live with. Foxes and wolves were not so different; they both belonged to the dog family, after all. The fox knew better than to fight the wolf, try to dominate him. Wolves were much larger than foxes, taller and heavier with a far broader snout and much heavier footstep. There were cosmetic differences, too, all in the foxes favor where beauty was concerned, but to his peril in a dog fight, as they made the fox more delicate. Besides, the wizard had no desire to end one of his own creations, especially one as fair as Cora's daddy.

The fox had an idea; wolves ran in packs, which was how the wizard could thwart the beast's murderous. If the fox could distract the wolf, if he could muster up a pack to run with, help the beast satisfy himself in the light of the moon and not the blood of the girl. It was more pack-like than the fox enjoyed, himself, but knowing the rush of the wolf pack, he called every wolf nearby in the surrounding woods, and they came. They came to meet their maker, run with the fox that made their world.

The moon blazed in the dark night till the razor's edge could be seen all around it, and the wolf pack ran against the empty black cover of night, swiftly, over endless miles of mountain prairie. Finally, the morning came, rounding the corner of the sky like a golden shower of light, and the wolves returned to their varied territories, turning to look behind them longingly on their way.

They left just the scattered man, shivering in the back of his own land, looking wild-eyed at the wizard who now sat calmly on a rock looking at him. The man was human again, covered in sweat, and alarmed by all he remembered. He recalled bursting into fur, howling at the moon, and he remembered the fox, the terrified child, his girl, scrambling to get away.

"Kill me," he said desperately to the wizard who straightened his pointy grey hat and smoothed his long white robe.

"I would sooner kill the star of this world than one such as yourself," the wizard replied.

"But what has happened? Who are *you*? Why did we turn into beasts and run wild in the light of the moon? I would have killed my own child!" The man's voice cracked and his wide eyes searched the snowy slope of his land. "If not for you, I would have."

"All is well now," the wizard said indifferently. "I cannot stay. There are forces still at work above." He pointed to the sky that now ruptured into soft white rays of early light, and he prepared to rise up with his walking stick in hand, into the blue, and higher still, into the outer hemisphere. He stood and, placing his foot on a rock, he stopped himself from pounding the stick and levitating, thinking what to say as a departing word.

"You will never see me again," the wizard said to the man, "and I won't see *you*. You'll return home and find the world as it was. I've corrected all that was wrong with your wife and daughter.

They are well now, but let me say this: you should keep up the good work, with your family I mean."

With that the wizard lifted himself into the air, allowing his form to go up, up, and upward still. He then expanded once he hit the stars, till he grew to full stature and stood before the three witches in the cave, with only the great caldron coming between them. The wizard lifted his hand and pulled Cora's world to himself. He drew it off the chain and across caldron, till he held it in his hand and tucked it under his right arm. He'd prepared for three streams of hate-filled magic blasted in his direction at once, but he managed to stop them with a word, masterfully drawing them into a conversation. Witches could hardly resist a witty exchange. "This is my world," he declared. "You had no right to take it."

"You," Izzy seethed, pointing her boney finger at the wizard. "You had no right to spend our share of the magic on Cora. You owe us, wizard, and you know it." She twisted her fingernail in the air, as if she'd jabbed it into his chest and punctuated her words with a twisting knife. Her sisters stood firmly by her side, and the three of them postured as a coven does, shoulder to shoulder, when an enemy threatens.

"And so I do," the wizard sighed, letting Cora's world fall into the deep side-pocket of his robe. He unbuckled his belt then, the very one he'd been adjusting on the mountain pass to cinch his coat, the day he tried to carry the world unfinished to the market. He cut the leather belt from the buckle and tossed it to Izzy, who seized it, holding it up with a gloating look in her eye.

Satisfied, she inspected it, and then clutched it to her chest. "This will do," she said.

"You stay away from my shop," he tried to bluff, tilting his head in a serious way and meeting each gaze with a stern glare.

"We want nothing with your shop," Lore said sweetly, and all three hags melted into remarkable young women, beauties in hoop skirts, with corsets tied snuggly around their waists. Their gowns were laced and sewn with gold beads. T he caldron disappeared as they sat daintily on a velvet couch, tucked with buttons. The wizard stopped to survey their gentle smiles, the smooth skin that replaced shedding flesh and wrinkles.

"You best keep to your home, wizard," Lore toyed with him, her long flirty eyelashes fluttering as she spoke. "Do try to avoid taking magic that isn't meant for you, brother."

"You may also want to avoid the passes in winter," Totem cackled, clearing her throat of the last of her toad-like croak. The aged tone of old wisdom and forbidden knowledge, that hags cackle, reminded the fox to be leery of beauty.

"I shall," the wizard agreed, looking through the veil the witches cast to blind him from their shriveled, twisted forms. He could not help admire their power, the work ethic they had to provide the evil that kept wizard's strong. He turned to leave, feeling their eyes follow him all the way back down the passage, back to the light of the entrance. When he stepped out into the Crooked Wood he could see the border, the brilliant hills of the Great Forest beyond it. The fox put Cora's world in his heart and shook one last dust of frost from his tail. He ran back to his great shop where the world would be hung with the others, to be finished properly and readied like any other world for the Spring Festival and the caravan of wizards across the pass, to the Market.

FRANCES ARCHER

At an early age, Frances discovered writing as well as a passion for social causes. Finding a love for writing poems and stories at home and school, and having written a letter to the editor of the local newspaper about "kindness to animals" at age 10, teachers encouraged Frances to join the Young Writer's Conference where she excelled and earned attendance at a national forum where she would come to know herself as a "writer."

To date, her work includes one children's book, *Edward Dumb as Ever*, that she is currently illustrating, and as a Child Mental Health Specialist, she has ambitions to complete more books for children to raise awareness of trauma in foster care and troubled families. Frances co-wrote a script called "The Bucket," which was adapted as a play and had wide success in church circles of several denominations in the state of Georgia. Frances is published in: Fort Benning's Family Life newspaper and on the Spokane Christian Counseling website, having written on various topics of family health. Her current projects include several memoirs, two fantasy novels, and one dark comedy.

*Note: art on pages 1 and 11 are by Frances Archer

WE

M. Kari Barr

We sat there, we sit here. We are and ever were. Like He who proclaimed: I Am; we are.

Wc think, we ponder, we communicate. Yet in this state we are limited, and so we wait.

My time arrived. I was observed, classified, and deemed worthy as was my other self. We are here now. Still, it is an eternal existence. Yet now we have language, whereas before, we simply were. My other self is female, I am male; like He who classified me. He brought me here. For His wisdom, I praise Him. For His charity; for offering me this chance—I adore him.

We received names! I am called Adiel. She is called Cherut. We received knowledge and glory in the beauty which surrounds us. We no longer merely exist in a space, which, one might say is seemingly empty and vast, while at the same time it is filled with an everlasting supply of beings like us, and more.

We view the creations of our Master, endless and eternal. They come and go. Bright stars and planets revolving around suns in eternal undulations of shifting colors. Peopled and teeming with botany and biology, power and love; all are lit with His power, glory, and light. Cherut and I are given free rein of our existence, we may explore the heavens, as it were, and any place ever created, or ever to be created. Where we are, all has been created, all is yet to be brought forth. One eternal now. It is a matter of desire and there we are.

Anywhen.

"Adiel, come look at this," Cherut calls with her lilting voice, like music to my ears. "Hurry, it won't last long!"

I hastened in time to see an exquisite green and mandarin hued blossom as it opened, exposed itself to the light, and sprayed forth its scent with a barely audible trill. We stood as witnesses to its sigh as it wilted, turning a dull olive and brown. It shriveled in Cherut's grasp having fulfilled its purpose.

"Mmm, that smells delightful. How would you describe that aroma, Cherut?" I ask as I take the limp flower from her hand.

She cocks her head to the side as she ponders, closing her eyes, blocking her misty green eyes from mine. She inhales to catch the last vestiges of that which had perfumed the air. "I would compare it to butternut squash paired with strawberry. Yet, softer."

We are standing within an opaque structure; white supports frame a myriad of octagonal panels making up the shell of the vast room. Plants of every kind grow from pots, troughs, and islands of land springing up from the floor.

“Will these be placed on a world one day?” I ask our tutor as he makes his way over.

He nods. “Yes, this lab, this garden is where we design many botanical elements to be used in all creation. It is endless and glorious. Have you determined yet that which suits your personalities?”

Cherut nods while I waffle. I turn to her—to learn of her desire.

“I would love to help in the creation of technology. I found working with electrons and light so very fascinating!” She beamed as though infused with the very light she adored.

I hung my head as that was not my desire. To be separated was unthinkable, yet I longed to work with the newly arrived like our guide. Not our tutor—his work would take eons to achieve. Like our guide, the one who greeted us when we arrived in this celestial sphere, I wanted to re-experience the same wonder and delight I had felt upon arrival through the eyes of those newly classified, to partake in their joy as they experience our new reality with touch, taste, sight and sound. All the wonders of our near corporeal beings.

Sensing my despair, Cherut took my hand and added, “But really, I want to do as Adiel desires. I want to be a guide for the newly classified.” Her gentle eyes looked at mine with love unbound.

And so began our division from being one; we.

In preparation for that which was to come, our separation was wisdom so far-reaching we were not to know of it for ages beyond that moment. We took that step together.

Our work as guides fulfilled my desire to witness joy for

ages as we shared our existence with the newly created. Cherut put her whole effort into it, but not her heart. Eons passed and I could not help but notice her eyes come alive as we shared with our charges the Technology Division.

I myself no longer felt the pull I once had for guiding. Change happens. I never suspected it could be so. Still, I did not share in Cherut's passion. But my love for her lead me to make a decision.

"Cherut, let us request a change in our duties."

That light within her gaze filled me with the joy I had been missing.

"Do you mean it, Adiel?"

I did. We addressed the proper overseer. He advised it would be considered. Not many days later we were contacted. But the news was not as expected.

"Adiel, you have been assigned a transfer to the planet in sector 1.1ZQA partition 46. You are to report immediately as a sudden replacement is needed for a failed transfer."

I smiled and asked, "And Cherut?"

"Cherut is to report to the Technology Division of Light and Sound."

Instantaneously I assumed Cherut would feel the same horror at separation that seized me. Turning, I witnessed a look of exultation beaming from her gentle face.

Seeing my fear she reached out a hand, "Peace, Adiel, all is as it should be."

"But how will I fulfill my purpose on that planet if you are not there?"

"Not all recombine as the same unit we began with."

It was true. I had witnessed countless separations. Some were even sent to different planets with no chance of meeting at all. I assumed that Cherut and I would arrive in the same city at the same time. I just knew our connection to each other would allow us to find one another. The thought of being without my other half filled me with anxiety.

Cherut took my hand in hers as we walked to the Light and Sound sector. Her joy was palpable even as she exuded sorrow. She too feared the separation, but to learn all she could within the technological field had truly been a longed-for hope. I determined to be happy for her; after all, that was why we requested to change departments. I wanted her to be happy. She had sacrificed her desires for me; for that I could leave her in peace with a positive outlook. Despite our separation, we would always be one.

Before saying goodbye, Cherut said, "Adiel, I love you. I do believe we will always be one. But remember this singular lesson we learned during our atomic structure class—a unit has value no matter how the structure is combined."

I was delivered to a family in a small town on a planet of moderate technological advancement. I report this now after I have completed that portion of my existence. While there, like most, I had no memory of my life before my birth. I grew and learned many lessons not available to beings before gaining corporeal temples of flesh. Appetites, temptations for that which degrades, and a yearning filled me—becoming far stronger as I matured.

I became a teacher. Opening the eyes of understanding to my young students gave me immeasurable joy. Science and art were my areas of focus. Still, I felt incomplete. Like part of me was missing. I courted a few women, but none ever seemed to be a perfect match.

As I pondered my lack, a phrase I often used in my lecture on atoms hit me with such force that I flung myself back onto my couch, resting my head upward so that I stared at the ceiling. "A unit has value no matter how the structure is combined." In class, I would go on to discuss gold and other metals. As a class, we would discuss the plausibility of something being made without atoms. Which would bring us back to the truth of my favorite statement, a unit has value no matter how the structure is combined.

But since I had been feeling rather depressed about missing my other half, as it were, I felt as if a light shone upon me, enlightening my understanding. *I would never find the "perfect" match. But the one I chose as a life mate would nevertheless have value.* This revelation freed me from anxiety. Dating became more fun; as a result I became more fun and enjoyable to be around. Changing my outlook created positive energy. That positive energy in turn became an attractant. Not too long after I made this shift in my outlook, I did indeed find a steely match to my magnet.

Tsandara was strong and beautiful, like the steel I came to associate her with. She stayed by my side through all the hardships and joys mortality offers. She held my hand as my true self left my temple of flesh. Not long after that I regained all my memories and I longed to know of Cherut's life.

She greeted me in our favorite garden. We were one. But I was incomplete.

Cherut told me about her experiences. "I spent ages learning everything I could in the Light and Sound Division. It was glorious and as wonderful as I had hoped it would be, though I did miss you. In time, I was sent to a planet far less advanced than the one you went to. My life was short, which is why I am here already. But in that time I helped the people of my planet advance. I discovered electricity and how to harness energy in batteries. It was exactly the life I wanted."

I told Cherut about my life, faltering when I came to telling about Tsandara. Cherut interrupted me, placing her hand on my knee, she said, "I remember that moment. I was allowed to witness your life for a brief time before I was sent to sector 1.1ZQA partition 85. We called our planet Erdd. Anyway, I was allowed to whisper to you; I reminded you of the value of any unit. I am so happy you found joy with Tsandara. I must tell you—I have linked my life with another as well. He is to arrive soon."

I had to wait a bit longer before Tsandara would joined me. Looking at my other self I smiled. "I love you too, Cherut. I forgot to tell you that before my birth. And you are wise. Thank you for helping me find Tsandara and allowing me to reach my full potential. Come, let's visit the gardens on our way to the science labs. I have some great ideas for my own planet."

And so it was that we two became two more. Moreover, neither were our partners linked with their other selves. Interconnected, we see we are all one family. United link by link we create a grand tapestry of noble metals—chain-mail extending into eternity.

We are one.

M. KARI BARR

lives in the Pacific Northwest near Spokane, Washington. Fantasy captured her imagination from a very young age, as did storytelling. At three she told her stories through collage, later—once she learned to paint—her works were representational pieces that told a story to her, even if no one else knew what that story was. Kari fully entered her career in writing in 2009. Her first novel entitled *Once Again: Tales of Destiny* is followed by book two in the series of six, *And Again: Tales of Destiny*. The series can be found online through popular book retailers.

Additionally, Kari writes picture books for young children; most notably her book *Thinktacular Thoughts* encourages creativity and interaction between a child's caregiver and the child. Readers can contact or learn more about the author at intangience.net.

Poem by M. Kari Barr

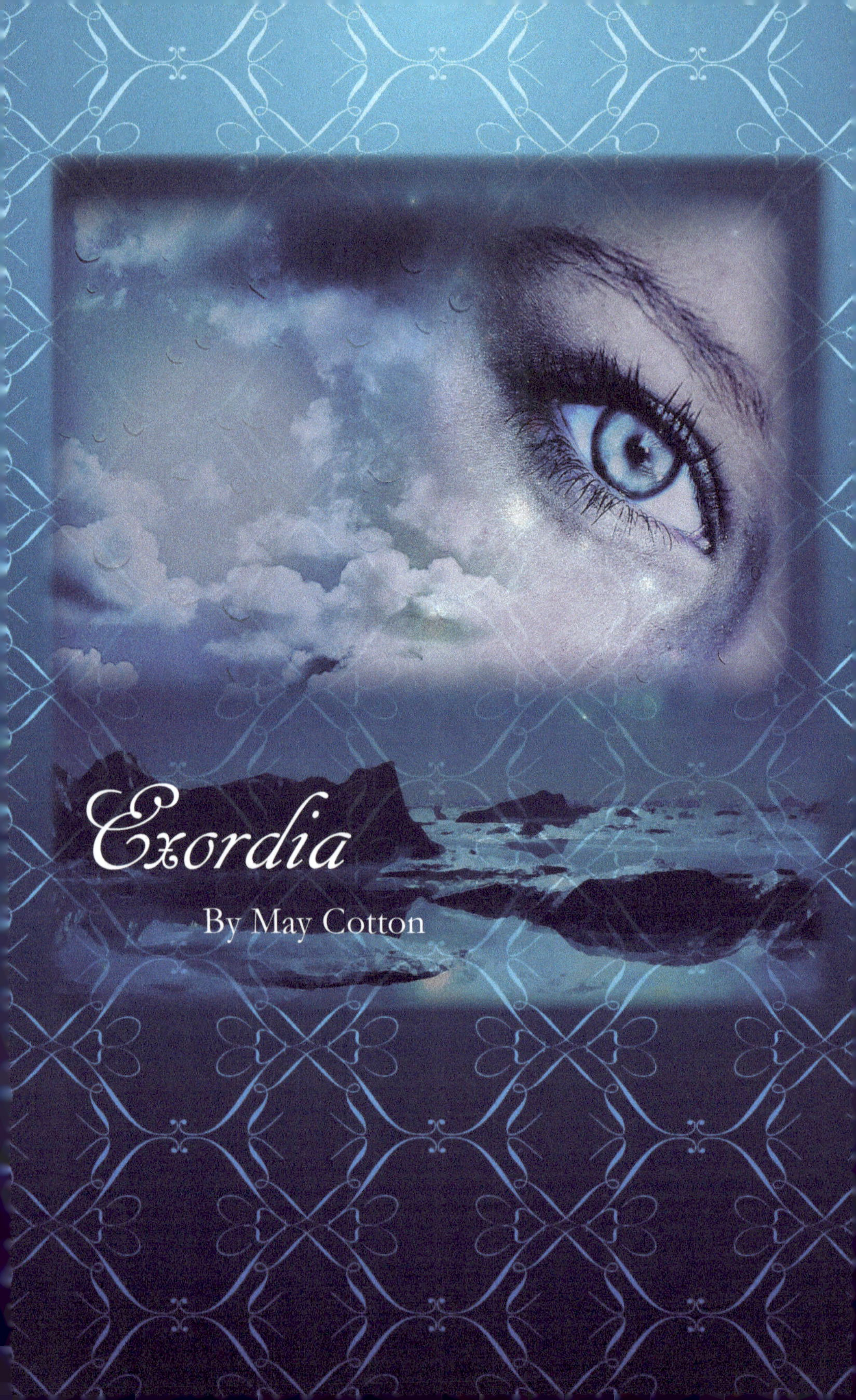
Exordia
By May Cotton

She awoke from a dream filled with colors, a catchy tune running through her head. Surprised, she began to hum and then to sing. As the music filtered through the air around her, the colors sprang to life, flitting, dancing, leaping about.

The tune tickled her toes and she wiggled them in the air. She stretched and giggled as she sang, flicking the colors from side to side. Trilling her voice, she cast colors up into the air where they broke into millions of tiny flailing creatures. Startled by her mistake, she quickly sang them wings, then watched as they flittered and fluttered, swirled and twirled through the air, searching for something on which to land.

She whistled up the greens and browns, teasing them into grass and trees, bushes and flowers. The flying things flitted about and then landed in the branches. Raising her voice to the blues, she coaxed them into droplets of water. Rain fell all about her, kissing the trees and flowers, gathering into streams and rivers, puddles and lakes. She laughed and splashed about until some of the water turned to vapor and drifted up to the sky.

Delighted by the vision, she flung her voice high, painting reds and yellows over the clouds. They flowed like fire and lit up the sky with their brilliance. Shivering with delight, she sang indigo up under the brilliance, muting the light. Then she closed her eyes and fell into a deep sleep.

When next she woke, she was surrounded by all sorts of odd shapes from her most recent dream. She looked around at all the flying things and saw they were hungry. The water was empty. Rolling up onto her knees, she fluttered her fingers in the water, making bubbles. Delighted, she dipped in with her toes and then splashed and swam around. Soon she was singing the bubbles into fish and other creatures of the sea, which were feeding on the smallest of the flying things while the hungry birds were feeding on the smallest of the fish.

Having fed her creatures, she turned her attention to the many shapes lying on the ground. Some were angular and some were rounded, but no two were the same. She pushed and pulled the shapes together into a plethora of furred and finned and winged critters, laughing and dancing as they evolved from foolish to silly and finally arrived at what she deemed practical. These she allowed to remain with her in the garden which was forming around them as she worked. She was pleased to find herself able to create so freely, without worry or care, without thought or plan. Eventually, though, she knew she was going to bring these creatures to life: they were far too precious to leave as mere images. The songs she'd sung the day before had no affect on the new creatures, but she enjoyed making them nonetheless, and when she had two of every shape and size she could imagine, she lay down and slept once more.

Awakening a third time, she realized there were now words on her lips, chants to give rhythm and direction to her songs. Now when she sang, there were commands behind the notes; she sang to her creatures, and the inert images she had made the previous day sprang to life. She took each pair aside and looked deeply into their eyes, singing a unique set of words to give each pair a special purpose. When all the pairs where assigned and scattered, she looked about at her garden and realized she was more tired than she had been after her previous two days.

The singing of the colors had been fun and delightful. The making of the creatures had been much harder. Bringing them to life, giving them each their assignments, had been most tiring of all. Folding herself into the comforting roots of a tree, she slept once more.

Now each time she woke, she played in the garden, gathering the abundance provided by the plants, sharing the bounty with the animals she had made. She spent weeks deciding what each pair should be named. Once her task was complete, each animal knew its own secret name and that of its partner, but none knew what the other animals were called. She wasn't sure why she did this, but it seemed important that each type of creature have its own language, its own culture, its own secrets.

After a while, she noticed that each pair of animals kept to itself, relying solely on its partner for companionship. Given long enough together, they produced offspring, and then the family kept to itself too. Few of her creatures were compatible, she realized, a curious commentary on her haphazard design. There had been no plan, only the pleasure of trying different things as colors and sounds and shapes came together in different ways. It had been immensely satisfying when each creation had become a living creature, but she had not considered how they might interact with each other. Perhaps it was just as well that the pairs all kept to themselves.

At last there was nothing left to do but tend the garden and feed the animals. First she became bored, and then at last she realized she was lonely. She did not belong to a pair like her animals who seemed to need only each other. As she wrestled with this problem, she wandered the garden, communing with the animals. But they appeared to only tolerate her, allowing her to fondle them but showing no affection back. She had created them to love only each other, to be partners to each other but not to others. She fell into a deep depression and retreated at last to the roots of her tree. Once again she was exhausted, but this time it was from sorrow rather than work. The tree received her lovingly and she passed into a long period of sleep.

This time she dreamed of a creature much like herself, one that went about on two legs instead of four. Like her, this creature had no wings, nor any other special attributes, except that it was different from her, in some way that drew her in. Even in her dream, she knew this creature was to be her partner, that, like all her animal pairs, this being would make her complete.

When she woke curled in the arms of a tree grown tall and thick over the long years of her sleep, she cast about for what she might use to create the partner-thing she had dreamed. She reflected on what she had been able to make from colors and shapes and song. But this recent dream left her no tools with which to create her vision. What could she use? She considered the earth, the plants, the water, the air, the lights in the sky. All these building blocks would give various characteristics, yet she wanted a *different* kind of creature to partner with her.

She thought and thought as she wandered through the garden, stroking a flower or whistling back at a bird. A 4-legged paced beside her as she walked, keeping her company, but reminding her again why she wanted a 2-legged like herself. Puzzling and pacing, she arrived back at her tree with a new understanding of where the partner must come from. Then reaching inside herself, she withdrew a piece of her own flesh, which she molded carefully with her hands and sang into substance and spoke to life.

The creature turned to look at her. As she looked deeply into his eyes, she saw that he was both of her and separate from her, which would forever bind them together in love and strife.

MAY COTTON

is the founder and moderator of **Not Your Mother's Writing Group.** She has been a serious writer since the age of 14, working out life's dichotomies through words. For many years she applied her BA in English as a technical writer and editor through her business *Dreamsmith Ink: Services to the Written Word.* Now retired, she focuses on her own writing, primarily memoir and essay, while dabbling in fiction and poetry. A fabric artist from childhood, she recently began creating with collage. She lives in Spokane, Washington, with her husband and cats, Pixel and Sadie.

Old Photo Albums

Most of these people mean nothing to me,

But this is my grandma, the girl in the tree;

Surrounded by blossoms big as her hands,

Up high on a sizable branch she stands.

One arm full of flowers, her radiant smile

Teases, allures; But her braids imply child.

She might be fifteen, though I'm guessing she's less,

How else could she climb up a tree in a dress?

Her elders would chide her were she a bit older,

The weight of adulthood draping her shoulder.

This is Amelia tender and free

Before childbirth and death knock her down from the tree.

My father survived her and passed me her genes;
And though he won't know it, he gave me her dreams.

May Cotton

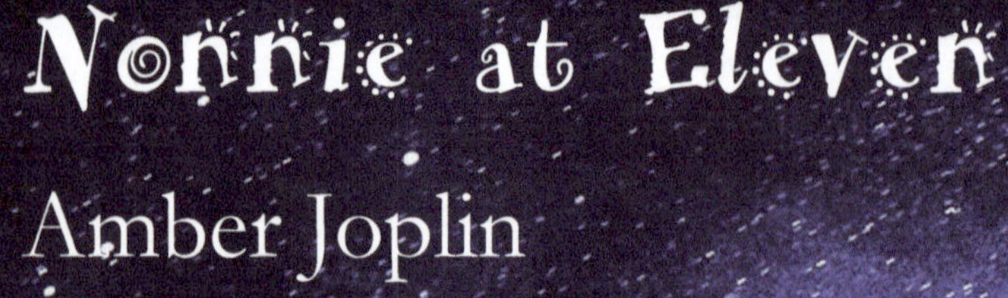
Nonnie at Eleven
Amber Joplin

CERTIFICATE OF TRANSLATION

I, Amber Joplin, am competent to translate from Axxyndomari into English, and certify that the translation of "Nonnie at Eleven" is true and accurate to the best of my abilities.

Translator's Preface:

I believe this story is the first to be translated from the Axxyndomari into English. As such, I found no precedent for representing unfamiliar Axxyndoma concepts. Thus, I have substituted Earth based concepts to represent Axxyndoma realities in an understandable fashion. Specific cases include, 1) time, including lengths of day and year. 2) Nonnie's schooling system, 3) her toys, such as the Easy Bake Oven, 4) names of body parts, and, 5) the family relationship between Nonnie and Mother.

Given my recent introduction to the Axxyndomari language I am indebted to Professor Aemennalea Yaeli of the Institute of Galactic Languages for her insight and encouragement. Also the Foundation for Universal Understanding for support during the translation period. My colleagues at Not Your Mother's Writing Group have challenged and sharpened my thinking. To all of these, as well as Ann Clayton-Jacob for her insight, I am profoundly grateful. What shortcomings remain are mine alone.

Further information on Axxyndoma and the Axxyndomari language may become available in time. Please submit specific questions to the translator.

Respectfully submitted, Amber Joplin, August 20, 2019

In the beginning, Nonnie was only eleven years old. Eleven years old and not allowed in the kitchen during the baking. She could hear Mother's voice still ringing in her thoughts, "Nonnie, you're not old enough to do our work. Please learn to be patient, dear. You are only eleven!"

Only? she simmered as she stormed away. *I'll show them what I can do with my Easy Bake oven!*

It wasn't the *real* Easy Bake oven. Nothing in Nonnie's life was *real.* Everything was all ideas and theories. She was tired of theories, she wanted to play with something real! She wanted to really, really make something.

So she said to her Not-Easy Bake oven, "Let there be a ball for me to play with!"

And there it was, a multicolored sphere floating up from the oven. She reached out and drew the ball closer. It was steamy and soft, with bits and pieces of crunchy looking things. It yielded to the pressure she put on it. *Putty,* she thought. *I'll call it Putty because it feels like I can put it in any shape I like.* As the putty began to cool, Nonnie set down her hot pads and took the ball into her hands, first tossing and then rolling it back and forth.

The thrill of holding and caressing her ball surprised Nonnie. She began to feel a strange new energy forming as she held and fondled her ball. A fire started deep within, roiling her insides, and spreading until every inch of her began to tingle with excitement. Her breathing quickened as she moved further back into her room, wanting to experience this amazing new sensation without being observed or interrupted. She loved the way her breath quickened, and the electricity arced along her skin. She drew the ball closer and closer, shaping and reshaping its surface gently.

Gently at first, then with more and more force, she dug her fingers into the malleable surface, reaching deep within the ball with both hands pulling and tearing, then squeezing and folding, then pulling again, and stroking. Stroking, she began to rub the ball against her body, feeling it spread out, warm and soft and growing.

She was in the ball. She was the ball and the ball was her. She was Putty.

Until finally it was over. The electricity began to fade away, no matter what she did. She was exhausted, deeply satisfied and deeply wanting more. She wanted to scream out her delight. She wanted to hold Putty close in secret. Totally confused, Nonnie laid back on her cushions. After a few moments she laughed. *No wonder her mother said she was too young to stay in the kitchen during the Bakes. Not too young for Putty,* thought Nonnie, *but far too young to see adults act as she had!* She giggled as she separated herself from Putty and gently reshaped the ball to fit under her pillow, then relaxed into a deep and restful sleep.

The next day Nonnie was distracted. She couldn't wait until she could be alone with Putty again. Tingles of the new fire teased her mercilessly, as did Zotir and Marena at school. They took turns asking, "Where are you, Nonnie?"

She jumped when Zotir playfully punched her arm. Nonnie wasn't ready to talk about Putty, so she just shrugged, and told Zotir she was trying to get away from his stupid jokes. The sad look in his eyes made her realize she needed to be more careful with her friends. A goddess of creation in training, she hated breaking things that someone else had made. She thought it would make her angry if someone damaged one her projects.

When she finally got home and away from the dinner table, where Mother had asked as well, "Where are you, Nonnie?" she ran to her room, pulled the door shut, and plucked Putty from under her pillow. No longer the steamy, soft ball, this ravished Putty had ridges and pockmarks—and dripped with water.

In order to see Putty better, Nonnie declared, "Let there be light!"

The space around Putty was flooded with the most amazingly beautiful light and she could see her ball was full of colors, blue, gold, red, brown, and gray. She spun Putty in her hands, exclaiming at the sparkle of light flashing off of the gold and white areas. She slowed the spin to examine designs etched in the surface.

Then she separated the light from the darkness to see the shadows that formed on mountainsides and in canyons. *What a beautiful ball.*

It was beautiful! Too beautiful to destroy! Nonnie realized she didn't want to crush it again. She held the ball delicately, spinning it at an angle on the tip of her forefinger and felt a fire of a different sort begin to burn in her. It was a sure knowledge that she had created something real and of value. Something good. Not something she would outgrow, but something she would work with and develop and cherish. A treasure she would protect. A jewel to shine in a perfect setting.

"Putty," she proclaimed, "you look most beautiful with the light moving across your surface." It was that splendid combination of half-light and half dark. "The light we will call *Day*, and the dark we will call *Night*."

Setting the spinning Putty carefully next to her bed, Nonnie lay back and watched the flashing colors whirl past until she dreamed. She dreamed of Putty growing and changing. She dreamed of strange creatures roaming the canyons and flying above the mountains. She dreamed of fish gasping for water, and birds falling to the floor of her room. In the middle of the night, she woke with a start to find tiny dragons, flopping fish, and strange oval-shaped shells collecting on the floor beneath the ball. Nonnie gently pressed the creatures back onto the ball, and rolled Putty through the shells to make sure she had gathered them all. The animals needed safe places to fly and swim, so she commanded the water, still dripping from Putty, to separate into sky waters and earth waters, and to cling to the ball.

When she woke again it was early and she had time to twirl Putty on her finger again, and admire the new white clouds floating above the ball. Intricate shadows fell across the surface as the clouds passed overhead. A thin film of water clung to the entire surface, making it sparkle. Looking closely however, she realized the biggest sea serpent had no place to swim. After a few minutes of thought, Nonnie told the waters to gather in the lower places and let the higher places become dried out. She named the largest water places *Seas,* and the dry places *Land.* She looked at her ball, and knew it was good.

Nonnie smiled as she prepared for her day.

That afternoon she was surprised to see how different her ball looked. The vast sea glistened in the light, but the dry land no longer sparkled. In fact, it looked quite exposed. The few birds that once soared over the hillsides, now hovered near the sea shore. Looking closer she realized all the animals were gathered along the shore line. Nonnie was stumped, she wanted the land to be an inviting habitat for the animals. She held Putty close and imagined different solutions. Could they make a cover that was beautiful and welcomed the animals? Then, hungry for her after school snack, she realized that Putty could be a garden with food for her creatures. "Can you grow things to eat that are beautiful?" she wondered aloud as she set Putty down.

Then she jerked back in surprise as a giggle emerged from the ball, followed by, "Silly girl, I am so full of life, I can grow you anything you can imagine."

"How can you be so full of life? How are you talking? I just made you in my Not-Easy Bake oven."

"Girl, you filled me full of your life the day you made me

and shaped me. I have your DNA buried in my depths and etched across my mountain ranges. I have a molten center of your passion deep in my core."

Nonnie faltered, sitting back on her bed. *What had she done?* Putty was alive and could talk. She was not simply a plaything. *What was she?* Nonnie buried her face in her hands, trying to think.

"What's wrong? Don't you like me anymore? You sure seemed to like me before!"

"I do like you, but I wanted a toy to play with, not something that laughs at me!" she snapped, suddenly needing to challenge this unexpected personality.

The giggle again. "Fine," continued Nonnie sharply, "I'm going to go have a snack, and if you are so smart, I want you to grow some plants to feed the animals. Make them pretty and yummy!"

Mother was in the kitchen and looked enquiringly at Nonnie, "How was school?"

"Fine." Nonnie bent toward her fruit cup, turning her face away from her mom. She grabbed the top book from the pile hoping for an escape. *Darn, it was How to Talk to your Pre-teen.* "This is a stupid book!" she blurted.

"Is it? Do you have some better ideas?" smiled Mother.

"No."

"Come on, Nonnie. What's going on? You haven't said more than ten words to me in the last few days!"

"I'm not ready to talk about it yet."

"Are you in trouble?"

"Maybe. No. I hope not."

"Let's go to your room then, and have a heart-to-heart chat."

Trapped, Nonnie slowly led the way.

***

"Mother, this is Putty. I made her in my Not-Easy Bake oven."

"Oh, Nonnie! What have you done?" Mother gasped.

"Isn't she beautiful? I made her, and then I shaped her, and then I dreamed the creatures. Now I am trying to make a good home for them. Putty is helping me!"

"Do you understand what you have done?"

"I made a real thing!" Nonnie struggled. "Can't you see that?"

"Yes, Nonnie, I see that very clearly. You made a real planet and you put life on it. How dare you do that at your age? Don't you know what that means?" Mother's voice quavered with emotion.

Nonnie cringed away from her mother. *A planet? Putty is a planet?* "I didn't mean to make a planet, just a ball to play with!" she protested.

"Your childhood is over. Now you must grow up and take responsibility for your planet!" Mother continued. "I had hoped you would have more time to be a child."

"I needed to make something real!" Nonnie screamed in frustration. "And I'm not a child!"

She pulled Putty close and turned away from her mother. "You can be mad, or you can help me, but I made Putty, and I will try to take good care of her." She was grateful Putty kept her silence.

"I will help you, Nonnie, but not tonight." Mother sighed as she left the room.

Nonnie was relieved they were alone again. Watching the spread of green across the land soothed her. *A planet! She had created a planet and had much more work to do!* Tentatively, she began to collaborate with Putty. She would imagine a smooth field of green in a valley, and when Putty generated the grasses, Nonnie would add blue, yellow, white, or pink flowers. She imagined shrubby plants and taller trees. She arranged them in clusters and in grassy spaces. It was captivating! Nonnie could change the colors and shapes of the plants and their fruits. She was thrilled with the process. "How am I doing, Putty?"

"How am I doing, Nonnie?"

She heard the giggle, and replied, "It's good. We're doing good."

They worked on the greenery until mother's sharp rap on the door signaled bedtime. That night Nonnie slept fitfully, waking now and then to wonder why her mother had been so distressed. *What had been so terrible about making Putty?* Her ragged dreams came one after the other as though in lines. Then it was as if the dreams were eaten by an ugly beast with a long nose and longer tongue. Turning away in revulsion, she witnessed swarms of disgusting worms and grotesque bugs begin to eat the new plants she and Putty had created. "No!" she screamed as she jerked awake. "Not the beautiful plants!"

"You've ruined everything!" Putty sobbed. "You dreamed up loathsome things and made me generate them! I hate you! This is all your fault!"

Nonnie hesitated. There was not enough time to get mother. "Stop it!" she snapped! "Don't act like a baby! I can't think with you blubbering like that."

Suddenly she knew. "It is my fault, but we can fix this! We need to make creatures to eat those bad bugs. Imagine balance. We can do this."

They worked together through the early hours harmonizing the needs of the plants and the animals. When it was time to leave for school Nonnie was exhausted, but exhilarated. She had imagined little flying mammals, colorful lizards with long tongues, and predatory insects like the dragonfly and lady bug. They had conceived more exotic birds, large and tiny, in every color. *Like flying flowers,* she thought. Together they had reversed the damage she had caused, turning Putty into a more enchanting creation.

Nonnie was also beginning to understand why her mother had been so upset. *This really was a big job.* She and Putty were so intimately connected that everything she did or thought affected Putty. Even her dreams were a hazard to the young planet. *How will I ever manage all of my thoughts—especially while sleeping? What will happen if I make a big mistake?*

At breakfast Nonnie was ready to ask for help. "Mom, I'm not sorry I made Putty, but I'm realizing that I can hurt her without meaning to. Can you teach me how to keep her safe?"

Mother smiled from under tired eyes. "I'll do my best to help you, Nonnie. I am sorry you made Putty, but I see you have done a beautiful job, and I am proud that you are taking responsibility for the life you have created. Putty can stay in your room for a few more days, and I will teach you how to shield her from unintended thoughts."

"But why can't I keep her?"

"Putty is not a toy, she's a planet. You see how much she has grown, and she will get much larger! She needs her place in the universe. Planets must feel sunshine and have visits from asteroids. They require neighbors, a moon, starlight."

"Can I go with her?"

"Yes, and no. Your heart and mind will always be with her, but your physical presence is too powerful to stay once we find her orbit. If you stay she will always cling to you rather than follow her star."

Nonnie gazed fixedly at her bowl. "This is really hard, Mom."

"Yes, it's the hardest thing about creating, releasing our creations into the universe. But it is the reason we are here."

After school, Nonnie went straight back to her room. She could hear Putty humming from down the hall. Her heart swelled as she caught sight of the planet. It had grown as they had added plants and animals. Now it half-filled her room and she had to duck underneath to get to her bed. She laid back and admired their work. "You are so amazing, Putty!"

"Thank you, Nonnie." and the giggle. "I'm having fun."

"I'm having fun too, but I learned that you need to have more than me in your life."

"Is there more?"

"Yes, much more! There is an entire universe of suns and stars and galaxies."

"What are suns and stars and galaxies?"

Nonnie was stumped. How to explain all that? "Let me put a thought in your mind, like an imagination, but don't try to make it."

Nonnie imagined the universe, spreading away, then brought suns and planets and galaxies into focus, like a planetarium show in her mind. "This bright clump is the Trilobite Nebula where stars are formed. Over there are the Seven Sisters, an open star group. See the smaller glowing shapes near that bright star on the left? Those are its planets, they go around their star. The white band of stars in the background is called the River of Milk. It's made up of more stars than we can count."

"Oh. It's so big!"

"Yes, it's huge. It's never-ending. Somewhere out there we will find the perfect place for you."

After a pause, Putty asked, “Are you sending me away because I said ‘I hate you’?”

“No, it’s not my choice. You are a planet and Mother says you need to live in an orbit around a star.”

“I don’t really hate you.”

“I’m glad you don’t. I know you were upset when you said that.”

“I think we make a good team.”

Nonnie smiled. She was surprised at the warm feeling that spread through her. “Thank you, Putty! I agree. We make a great team!”

Thursday, Nonnie and Putty worked on a system for watering the plants. Putty had noticed that when she spun, wind patterns moved the clouds which had formed over the sea onto the land. She thought that if the clouds could drop their water onto the land, the plants would have the moisture they needed to grow. After school Nonnie spun Putty faster and slower until they found the perfect speed for rain to fall. As raindrops fell onto the dry land, some of it soaked into the dirt, but much of it trickled down slopes and pooled in depressions. When these pools filled, water overflowed and cascaded down hills and through valleys collecting in larger and larger streams, all the way back to the sea. Nonnie was delighted at how the pools and streams of water enlivened the land. “Look,” she exclaimed, “the animals are exploring the streams! Maybe they will find new homes closer to their food.”

Putty kept growing and by morning huge stress fractures appeared along her shore lines and across the great land mass. The land masses began to separate and drift apart on Putty’s core of molten lava. The sea rushed in between the land masses and Nonnie woke to see huge clouds of steam rising in magnificent plumes.

“Did I do that?” she asked. “I don’t remember dreaming about steam.”

“No, I think I’m just growing up.” Putty replied.

Before she left for school, Nonnie helped Putty rearrange the continents. They moved tectonic plates under, over and past each other, raising up new mountains and forming valleys. As the continents moved, lava escaped through Putty’s crust.

“Wow, that feels really good!” shouted Putty as another explosion of lava rocked her ocean floor. “I feel so much less stressed now!”

“I love that string of islands you just finished making!” Nonnie responded. “What a great way to reduce stress!”

“I didn’t realize how tense I was feeling. I guess I really am afraid to go out into the universe,” confessed Putty, as she began to cover the islands with coconut palms.

“I’m scared too, I still haven’t learned how to keep you safe when you move out. And I will really miss you!

“You will? You won’t just make another planet and play with her?”

“No, I don’t want another planet. I want to learn to work with you in your star system. We have had so little time together, but I already know that you are very special.”

“I am?”

“You are my first real creation. I didn’t know what I was doing, and I was so excited the day I made you that I put all of myself into the experience,” replied Nonnie thoughtfully. “Now that I know how important you are to me, I will be more careful to keep a safe emotional distance with the planets I make when I grow up.”

“What are you saying?”

“You are deep in my heart. You feel like a part of me. I think that means I love you.”

Friday evening Mother came to the bedroom. “Well, you don’t look like a new planet!” she exclaimed. “You look very developed and experienced! It takes a typical planet millions of years to have so many features!”

Putty glowed, “Thank you, I feel young, though.”

Mother laughed. “Enjoy the feeling while it lasts. Tomorrow Nonnie and I will take you out to look at some orbits. I see you already have a spin.”

“Yes, we worked out the spin two days ago. It manages the winds so we have rain over most of the land. We haven’t figured out how to make the oceans more active, though,” added Nonnie thoughtfully.

“We will find a moon. A moon will pull the oceans back and forth and keep your oceans waving.” said Mother. “It’s an old trick!”

The next morning after breakfast, Mother and Nonnie pulled on their traveling gear and reached their arms around Putty holding her between them. Mother imagined Putty out of the room and they were off. Mother would imagine a sun and they would be there, looking for the perfect orbit. They visited famous stars like First Warrior and the Wolf Stars, but Nonnie thought they were too crowded. They traveled to the Hunter Nebula to look for a new star, but Putty felt she looked too old to be with a new star. Then Mother remembered a small solar system in the River of Milk that had a space for a planet.

When they arrived, Nonnie and Putty smiled.

“Oh, yes,” whispered Putty, “this looks like a good home for me.”

Around a lovely yellow star whirled eight planets all in different shades of brown, yellow, red, orange and blue. One planet had rings. Another orbit was filled by a field of debris.

"What happened there?" asked Putty.

Mother checked her readout. "This system formed with enough material to make the ninth planet, but that huge planet out there kept the mass from collecting. We can use some of the debris to make a moon for you. This star is rated for nine planets, so you will fit right in." She adjusted a setting on her device. "Nonnie, please test where the light levels are best."

Nonnie struggled with the meter, trying to remember what she had learned in optics class. "The light between the yellow planet and the red planet is very close to the light I used in my room and has a good temperature range."

"What name do you want to use in the Galactic Registry?" Mother asked.

"What do you mean?" asked Nonnie. "Her name is Putty."

"Putty is a good nick name, but it's not really suitable for a significant planet in this solar system, and potentially in this galaxy. She needs a formal name."

"I've always liked the name Marris," said Nonnie. "It means from the sea. Do you like it, Putty?"

"Marris," Putty repeated slowly. "I like it."

Mother checked the register. "Great! That name is available." Then, speaking into the device, "Requesting permission to install Marris Ninova as third planet from Solis, River of Milk galaxy."

"She gets my name too?" asked Nonnie excitedly.

"She is a planet of your creation and will always be known by your name." replied Mother.

“Your name is Ninova?” asked Putty. “I thought it was Nonnie.”

“Nonnie is my nickname. Ninova means home, so your new name is perfect. It means home in the sea!”

Just then permission came through to install Marris. Mother and Nonnie once again linked arms and Mother showed Nonnie how to visualize the orbit Marris would follow. Together they gently swung the still growing planet into her place in the universe.

Nonnie and Mother pulled back to watch Marris begin to circle her star. At this distance Marris looked almost like the two day old Putty that Nonnie had first seen in the *morning after* light. “She is so beautiful.” Nonnie sighed.

“Yes, she looks like a pearl out there floating against the black velvet sky. You made a lovely planet.”

“I can feel her in my heart and in my mind. Can you teach me how to stay very close and keep her safe?”

“Remember the bond you have and how it felt when you first made Putty. Focus on the connection. Now focus more.”

Just then she heard a whisper inside, “Nonnie, I’m flying! Can you see me?”

And she whispered back, “Yes, Marris. I see you! You look amazing!”

Mother continued, “If you practice your focus, soon you will be able to hold it constantly so Marris can tell you if she is lonely or needs help. You will also need to come to the area from time to time to observe the surroundings and push away dangerous objects.”

“I want to come every Saturday!” Nonnie replied excitedly.

"That's best," replied Mother. "There is something happening with Marris that makes me think you need to keep a close watch on her. She has the aura of a goddess of creation. She will produce very interesting creatures. You may need to protect her from them as well as the greater universe."

Nonnie wasn't worried. *The aura of a goddess of creation! What could go wrong?*

AMBER JOPLIN

loves stories and credits them with shaping her understanding of human behavior. After finishing her doctoral studies in environmental design, she joined Not Your Mother's Writing Group to transition from academic writing to telling stories which inform and engage. Her writing ranges from whimsical explorations of alternative realities to deeply personal examinations of environmental impacts on well being.

Poetic Photo Art by Amber Joplin

Gnomes

TERESA KELLY

CHAPTER 1

Sally breathed out a grunt of relief and dropped the final box of garbage on the pavement. Her eyes were smarting from the sweat pooled below her eyes under her fogged lenses. She stretched her aching back, hearing phantom popping from vertebrae and joints. Relief at getting this part of the job done faded when she turned back to the house. Her mom's house.

The rosy brick of the cottage glowed where the last of the day's light caressed it. A worn door of faded green, centered behind a crisp white railed porch, took on warmth in the fading sun. For a moment Sal could see the charm of the place before grief shadowed the image.

She had never visited her mom's new home while Mom had been alive, in spite of numerous invitations. Life always seemed to intervene and tentative plans had been put off. Sally shied away from her memory of Eric, intervening with plans, convincing her to delay her visit.

Sal sat down abruptly on the low stone wall enclosing the front garden. A wave of feeling crushed her. Why had Mom moved away from Portland anyway? Regret, anger, loneliness were all mixed in there with a jumble of other emotions she hadn't put a name to yet.

She'd mostly been numb since she got the call. Irritation flared when 'Mom' had popped up on her phone. It was the middle of her work day and Mom knew not to call at the office. Sally winced, hearing her curt greeting echo in her memory.

"Hey Mom, I'm working. Make it fast." She wedged the cell against her cheek with her shoulder while she sifted through a pile of papers on her desk.

"Is this Sally Anderson? Doris Anderson's daughter?"

A frown pinched Sal's brows together. *Why is this woman calling me?*

"Yes, this is she. Who is this?" Her voice slowed as her heart quickened. Reasons a stranger might call on her mom's landline began to pop into her head.

"I'm sorry, so sorry to call you like this. Your mom—"

"What about my Mom? Who are you? What's happened? Is she hurt?" Sal's words tumbled out in a wave of panic. She didn't recognize the harsh voice as her own.

"I'm a friend of your mom's, her next door neighbor, Eleanor. She might have mentioned me? She's gone, dear. I'm so sorry."

"Gone? Gone where? What are you saying?" A sob tried to force its way out of her throat but she refused to allow it. This wasn't happening. It couldn't be real. She had just talked to Mom a few days ago.

"She passed away last night. When she didn't meet me for our walk this morning I came over and—" The woman cleared her throat before continuing. "We have each other's key for emergencies—"

"I don't believe you. This is a mistake." Sally wanted to lash out, hurt this stranger who was changing her world forever.

The woman didn't raise her voice but it seemed to ring in Sal's ears like an enormous bell. "The EMTs said she had a massive heart attack and died instantly, some time in the early morning. They said she didn't suffer."

The words flailed Sally relentlessly, the details explained by the compassionate voice chipping away her wall of denial until it crumbled inside.

Sal ended the call, but not before a terrible cry ripped from her throat. When her cell rang again moments later she threw it across her office.

***

Sally became aware she was crying, sitting on the stone wall in front of her mother's house, because it wasn't sweat pooling under her eyes and steaming up her glasses. She surreptitiously wiped her eyes and nose on a corner of her ragged sweat shirt before getting up to hurry toward the house. If Mrs. Dawson, that Eleanor, saw her, she would try to help, and Sal couldn't bear to be around her. She knew she wasn't being fair, but she hadn't the strength to overcome her aversion to the woman.

Her quick exit derailed when she tripped over a small package at the front door. Arms windmilling, she managed to catch herself before she fell by grabbing the door frame. Her toes throbbed and she wiggled them inside her tennis shoe, hissing at the pain. The box was small and had been there when she arrived. She kept reminding herself and then forgetting to bring it in. Stooping to pick it up, Sal was sure it had been against the wall in the corner of the porch while she had been trekking out loads of garbage. Now it was in front of the door. She grunted with effort trying to lift it. No wonder her toes hurt, the package was heavy!

She braced it awkwardly against her chest while fumbling the door open with one hand. Carrying it to the kitchen table, she let it slip through her fingers to land with a dull thud, creating an echo through the empty house.

There was no label except the word Sunny scrawled across it—her mom's nickname.

The package was oddly shaped. She picked at the top and pulled away layers until a bright red cone poked out. Someone must have left this at the door, and when Sal failed to bring it in, they must have moved it in front so she would see it. *How had I missed tripping over it or at least seeing it while I hauled load after load of junk to the curb this morning?* She started to rip more of the brown paper off the package when a sudden thought had her eyes searching for the kitchen clock. The face of the funky black cat clock, eyes rolling in time to the swinging tail, declared it was almost noon. Frantically, she checked her phone but the time agreed within a few minutes. The funeral was at one but she was supposed to be there at least a half hour early.

Sal tried to remember her last shower but drew a blank. Probably the morning she had flown to Oregon, she thought, three days ago. She ran her tongue over her teeth, the faint fuzziness indicating she had not brushed them this morning. Her hair lay flat and greasy on her head. She'd been wearing the same ragged school sweatshirt and jeans since she arrived, except when she met with the funeral director and minister to plan Mom's memorial service.

Rushing to the bathroom, she started yanking off her clothes. Sal turned on the shower and dug out her mom's hair dryer. There was no flat iron and she wasted time searching for her own in her unpacked suitcase. Since she was there, she dug out the suit, blouse and shoes she planned to wear to the funeral. No time to iron so she hung up her clothes and took them with her into the small bathroom beginning to turn steamy.

Twenty minutes later, her hair mostly dry, minimal makeup on, she was trying to pull black hose over damp legs and poked a hole with her a nail, causing a large run down one leg. Discarding them, she finished dressing. Her bare legs weren't too bad, although she hadn't taken time to shave them. Sally looked at her cell again. She was going be late.

Her lips quivered when she saw there were no phone messages or texts from Eric. Moments later she was out the door, the partially opened package forgotten on the kitchen table.

No one was there when the rustling of paper disturbed the quiet of the kitchen.

CHAPTER 2

The women rang the doorbell although they expected no answer. Just to be sure, they knocked before using Eleanor's key to the house.

"Oh my," said the first one through. The rest crowded behind her, a group of five women who had sacrificed attending the service to prepare Sunny's house for the after-funeral gathering. They'd expected to lay out the food and do some clearing up in the living room and kitchen.

Sunny had been a relative newcomer to the community, moving almost a year ago from the coast, but she had gathered friends quickly. Her housekeeping had been average, complicated by her tendency to collect any choice items that came her way. Sunny had been an avid garage sale and thrift store shopper, adept at finding lovely things for a pittance. Her friends got used to shifting things out of the way—beautiful, useful things, but still an overabundance creating an obstacle course out of the small cottage. The surfaces in the living room were neat as a pin, every space was empty except for the shelving lining the room with old books in faded leather bindings. A bunch of flattened boxes dropped from one lady's hand breaking the spell.

"The daughter must have been working like a fiend to clear this place out," said one plump fifty-ish woman with a stylish pixy cut, colored an unlikely red.

"Where do you suppose all her stuff is?" questioned another. As one unit, they scampered down the hall, checking out the small bedrooms. Sunny's room was clean and neat except for the suitcase laying open on the bed, a few clothes scattered across the bedspread. The other two bedrooms were packed. Moving boxes were stacked floor to ceiling, blocking the furniture and windows. The women wanted to poke around more but they needed to start setting up in the kitchen.

"If all of the serving dishes are packed, Gail can run home and get what we need." The oldest woman, Mrs. Mendez, was deceptively frail looking until you looked into the fierce eyes of a general. Gail nodded agreement, although she blustered inside, *Why do I have to do it?*

A quick survey showed the kitchen was still in its normal confused clutter. There were plenty of dishes and serving spoons.

Directing her minions, Mrs. Mendez quickly got them organized, sending two women out to unload the cars. They had brought plain white cocktail napkins, paper plates, cups and plastic utensils plus a few late flower arrangements from the funeral home.

One of the two remaining women started dusting and straightening the living room although there was little to do there. The other prepared a couple of boxes and started wrapping newspaper around the countless crocks, jars and other curios littering the kitchen counters.

The kitchen table was clear except for a garden gnome nestled in brown paper.

"You need to join your friends outside," Mrs. Mendez said, lifting the gnome with some effort and carrying it out the back door.

It was just her fancy when she heard a "yes, please" in a small squeaky voice as she cradled the little man.

CHAPTER 3

The sky began to drip rain when Sally came out of the chapel. She stood in it a moment dumbly, before a helpful stranger covered her with his umbrella and ushered her to her mom's car. Then she was parked at the curb of Mom's house, barely aware of the drive, staring as cars parked and double parked up and down the street. Men and women poured into the cottage carrying covered plates and dishes, flowers from the funeral (she had forgotten about those) and folding chairs.

Sal recognized a few people from the funeral and realized what was awaiting her. A gauntlet of strangers who would tell stories she didn't know about her mom, question why they hadn't met her before, commiserate with her, and force emotion from her if they could.

She couldn't face it. She started her mom's Buick again, but the cars around her blocked her in. Feeling trapped, she grabbed her purse, catching the strap on the gear shift and spilling contents on the seat and floor. Abandoning it she opened the door but it was too late. An older couple waited for her, umbrella sheltering, hand on elbow guiding, guiding her up the steps and through the front door. Into hell.

Her stony response to the people surging around her gained her some space.

Eventually, they left her alone except for periodic encounters with awkward expressions of condolence trotted out from shopworn sympathy cards. *If one more person says Mom was in a better place I am going to scream!*

Mrs. Mendez bustled up, the crowd parting automatically for her. She carried a plate loaded with several types of salad—potato, macaroni, and pea—creating small landslides over slices of ham and turkey. A roll, soggy in one corner from salad dressings teetered perilously on the edge. Sal's stomach flipped greasily; she gave the woman a tight smile when she accepted the plate, afraid to open her mouth, certain the few bites of toast from breakfast would spew out.

Patting her tightly coiled white curls against the side of her head, the old lady said, "I wasn't sure what you liked, Deary, so brought you a bit of everything." She frowned, eyes narrowed, then snapped at one of her lieutenants. "Get this child some punch. She must be parched." Turning back she patted her hair once more, smiled in a way that reminded Sal of a shark approaching its victim before marching away.

Sally sat on the couch, nodding to those who stopped, avoiding eyes or a touch when possible, the punch in the clear plastic cup going warm in her hand. The noise dropped, softened, then slowly died away except for the clink of dishes in the kitchen.

Four women filed through the living room, murmuring sounds while she bobbed her head like one of those toys. Mrs. Mendez followed with her gimlet eyes surveying the room and picked up a last abandoned cup. The old lady said a goodbye bracketed with endearments before following her little group of workers.

There was a faint sound of voices outside; they died away and she was alone.

Sal lifted the untouched plate from her knee, careful to support the bottom when the softened paper tried to slide food to the floor. Her other hand still held the warm punch. She walked to the kitchen; it was spotless. Someone had even emptied the trash cans she saw when she dumped her plate and cup into a pristine garbage bag liner.

She stood there, staring at the sparkling counters, empty of her mom's treasures, the ones she'd planned to pack after everyone left. What was left? She had to do something.

Eric should have been there. She had been so numb over her mom's death it took several days before she realized Eric wasn't coming with her. He never offered and when she tentatively asked him to come, he explained in his patient voice why it was impossible. The same patient voice he'd used to neatly derail her plans time after time to visit Mom. Sal would love to blame Eric. It would be easy, but she had gone along.

"Oh, Mom, what am I going to do?" The words burst out of her and Sal realized they had been hovering there for days.

Her body started to shake and she burst out crying. Not the slow drip of tears periodically sneaking upon her since she lost Mom. She was really crying, bawling. Wailing like a banshee in pain, a pain she wasn't sure would ever go away.

Sal walked blindly toward the kitchen table and sank down, cradled her head in her arms and let the grief carry her where it willed.

CHAPTER 4

Sal dreamed. She was somewhere, not in darkness or light, cocooned in warmth, like love made tangible. A mix of rosewater and breath mints scented the air and she knew it was Mom before she turned and was held in her arms. Mom's lips moved, like one of those silent movies. Sal strained to hear and to speak. The arms still enclosed her and though Sal was a head taller, she felt safe and comforted. Understanding and unconditional love flowed from her mom without words, and Sal clung tighter, trying to express her regret and her love, grateful for the chance to say goodbye. Then the dream evaporated and she hovered above herself as she slept with her head in her arms on the kitchen table. Her eyes were closed and the strain in her face had smoothed. Unease tickled the edge of Sally's awareness. A dark figure bent over her, gesturing. She sensed lips moving but again, no sound. The figure leaned closer and whispered silently with a breath of air on her ear. A sense of urgency, of danger, spiked through her and she woke with a jerk. Her heart beat a frantic alarm in her chest. The image of the looming figure was etched on her open eyes for a moment; then she blinked and it was gone.

She was alone. Shadows cast by the moon filled the kitchen, flowing into the room through windows framing the backyard. The dimness leached all of the color from the world, leaving behind shapes of silver and gray. Time stretched painfully like a distorted rubber band and then snapped back into place. Her heart slowed. She became aware of the crick in her neck and shook out the numbness in her arms where her head had rested.

Just a nightmare, she calmed herself, rubbing her face and tired eyes. A creaking noise startled her and she tensed in the chair. A feeling crept through her—she was not alone.

The noise came again and she saw the kitchen door move slightly. A touch of wind brushed her cheeks. This time she firmly set her fears aside. The kitchen door must have been open all night while she slept, hinges protesting when the door was gripped by a gust.

Sally sucked in a breath, feeling weariness swallow her. She was at her mom's place—and Mom was gone. She needed real sleep; she couldn't continue this way. When she arrived the other bedrooms had been full of objects cluttering every surface, including the floor, so she had reluctantly put her stuff in her mom's room. She supposed the neighbor and friends had cleaned the bedroom. It was tidy with fresh sheets and bedding. Even the bric-a-brac on the dressers and side tables had been dusted. But something kept her from sleeping in the room. There was an elusive hint of corruption, a nasty smell lingering under the plug-in air fresheners. What rest she'd managed after working herself exhausted had been on the overstuffed couch in the living room.

She realized the crushing weight of grief and regret was missing and waited but it didn't come. Calm filled her, filling in the edges and smoothing out the sadness until it was forced away into the background. She remembered her dream of Mom, hugged it to her. Sadness would fill her again, but Sal thought the bitterness would never be as bad. The calm seemed almost unnatural but the relief was too seductive for her to resist, even if she could. Her hands lay flat against the tabletop now, and she watched them, knowing they would have been shaking uncontrollably except for this blanket of peace.

The door creaked again and she rose from the table, pushing up with those curiously steady hands. Walking to the door, she stepped out on the narrow back porch. The light of the moon seemed like a living thing, more real than the world it caressed. She felt it go through her, as if her flesh was transparent. She kicked off the sensible black pumps she'd worn to the funeral and stepped down. The tickle of cool moist grass under her feet welcomed her and she paused to dig her toes into the soil. The light drew her on, into the center of the small lawn and she turned her face up to the almost full moon hanging like an oval paper lantern in the sky. A six foot cedar privacy fence, grey with age, softened with a mix of firs and dwarf fruit trees, encased the pool of light. Silence wrapped tightly around her. She dimly wondered at it. There should be some noise in this heavily populated neighborhood. A sense of anticipation rose beneath the calm. She felt poised on the brink of some great and wondrous event.

A squeaky voice sounded at her feet, "We need to talk."

CHAPTER 5

She looked down and saw a little man with a tall pointed cap angled cockily over one eye. His nose bulged over a wide, grinning mouth showing wide blunt teeth and arms rested akimbo on small hips. She had the impression of gay colors stifled to grey by the moon's feeble lamp. The top of his pointed cap barely reached her knee.

"Are ye deaf then?" he said. "We don't have much time."

I am dreaming, Sal thought, kneeling in the grass before the garden gnome come to life. The calm surrounding her frayed, she shuddered when one of his little hands reached out and tugged at her shirt. With a cautious finger she touched his jacket at the shoulder. The texture was rough like stone and almost as firm when she pressed.

The little man's, *the gnome's*, breath huffed out in a frustrated sigh. "Ye humans are so caught up in the look of things. Do ye not know there is more to something than the surface?" The hands were fisted again and resting on his hips. A rustle of grass told her one boot was slowly tapping.

"It would be a help if ye would carry me to the house. I do not move so swift in this form."

He was heavy. Sal staggered a moment before walking back to the porch. She carefully set him on a white metal table before sinking into the wicker chair flanking it. Her eyes were only a little higher than his after she sat and watched, fascinated, when he winked at her with one large eye as his little hands adjusted his cap.

"Do you have a name?" Sal's voice came out in a hoarse croak. She hadn't spoken since she woke, she realized.

"That would be tellin', now wouldn't it," the small man said, rubbing at his chin with a rasping sound. "Ye can call me

Oakheart, if ye would, and you'd be Sally, the light of your mum's eyes."

"How did you . . . did my mom know about you?"

"In a way. She was sensitive, not like you, but receptive. Once she had accumulated several of us—but nay, I should be starting at the beginning." He pondered a moment, the rasping noise of his hand to his chin loud in the small porch. "We were guardians, protecting the folk within our care from evil influences. We perched on top of city walls, castles and churches and kept The Enemy at bay."

"What, like gargoyles?"

"Exactly like gargoyles!" His voice had deepened and snapped out his response. He seemed to settle himself a moment before continuing. "We were spirits, minor angels, sent to help humankind rediscover the divine during terrible times in their history."

"You mean the Dark Ages." The story was sounding phoney to her, like his accent that seemed to come and go. *But then again, I am sitting here talking with a yard ornament, so who am I to judge?*

"Yes, we worked to protect humans then, but we also protected many other places and times, the palaces of Emperors of China and Japan, temples in India, libraries of the Moors and many other places as humans faced the threats of invasion, disease, and hunger.

"As times improved, the need for us, the belief in us, eroded and we started to fade. Just a few at first, leaving the shell of themselves behind. When enough of us were gone, The Enemy was able to penetrate our defenses and destroy those of us who were alone and isolated, using humans as its tools. Alerted, we tried to renew our defenses, but we were too weak."

Sal didn't speak, but reached out to touch his small shoulder gently, in sympathy with the agony of sorrow leaching from his voice.

He bobbed his head a moment before continuing. "Most of my people lost the ability to change form; only the strongest of us were able to flee."

"I've seen gargoyles, statues from China and other places, plus tons in pictures."

"Just the shells, my dear. Or copies in stone or concrete. One of us stumbled upon a yard with a small stone figure of a man, seeming to guard the small space and he copied it, sending out word to the others. The small shape took little energy and was familiar enough for all of those remaining to assume the shapes. We were scattered but for many years hidden.

"Who's this Enemy?"

"He has many names but is the essence of evil and corruption and he hates all life, even as he uses humans to destroy it and themselves."

"Tell her about her mother." A new voice spoke. It was deep, and strangely familiar, causing her to jump in her chair when it intruded into their conversation.

Oakheart harrumphed deep in his chest but didn't answer. A creaking came from the stairs and she saw a small stone dragon laboring up the porch steps. It was dark with light colored chips where parts of the surface had broken away. A stylized dragon, with a long tongue curling out and up between stone fangs, its wings folded back along its sides, one only a broken stub. It was half the height and bulk of the gnome, with an odd sneer lifting the lip on one side of its open mouth.

"Tell her what happened, or I will."

"About my Mom? She was helping you, you said." Sal felt a

chill that didn't come from the night air.

"Yes, she was a good person. We wove wards around the house, but when she left, we couldn't protect her."

"I don't understand. She died in bed from a heart attack." Something crept up her body, a coldness freezing her insides.

"Your mother brought it inside herself, a fancy she bought at a yard sale. It worked on her while she slept, twisting her thoughts and spirit night after night, right under our noses."

"I felt it," the broken dragon said. He'd reached the porch deck and was crossing it slowly with a dragging sound. A spicy scent filled the air with a hint of musk, a scent she would have drawn in with pleasure but for the ice enveloping her soul.

"I changed and watched through her bedroom window on many nights. Only on the night she died did I discover it. A small wooden cat, curled asleep on her bedside table turned to a black mist and floated to her bed, wrapping around her face and head. I broke through the glass, losing some of my essence—." He drew attention to his broken wing with a flex of its stub. "It panicked and started to enter her nose and mouth. I tore it away, but she was choking and gasping for breath so some remained inside her. The stuff in my hands fought me, burning away at my surface attempting to get free. I held on and tried to use my breath to draw away the rest but I was too late. I don't think she awoke. I'm sorry."

"Why? Why would it kill her? Why is it after you?" Sal edged away from them in her chair. Whether from the fantasy of their existence, or the words hammering through her heart, she wasn't sure.

"She was helping us, unknowing, gathering us together, those in reach. We are a ghost of what we were, most of us unable to change, or speak or move in our current state.

But together, we can guard and protect and keep out evil," said the gnome, holding out his arms.

"But you didn't. You didn't take care of her."

The gnome dropped his arms and lumped. "She brought something in, somehow, the enemy slipped it past us. It may have been here a time before it was awakened."

"I thought you said the Enemy used humans," she accused, her breath starting to hitch.

The dragon spoke, "It isn't common but the Enemy can send his minions directly, on occasion, but it weakens him for a time." Shifting toward the gnome he said, "Now tell her the rest."

"The moon will be full in two nights and it will be a clear night," said the little man. "Moonlight strengthens us. The weaker conserve their energy for this full moon. The strongest as well. They waited only for me. I am to be the gate, a gate to new life."

"I will be your guardian," said the dragon to Sally. "I will protect you until our folk can escape." The small dragon shifted closer and she stifled a hysterical laugh.

"Why guard me? Why are you telling me all this?"

"Something still lingers in the house. I can't pin it down, and you packing up most of her treasures hasn't helped." The dragon's sneer twitched deeper with irritation.

"We need two things," Oakheart interrupted. "First, we need the malignant influence removed from the property so we can seal the perimeter against The Enemy. Second, we need your help gathering the last of our folk who made it to this area."

"You get my mom killed, but you need my help? Why should I help you? What's going to stop me from getting in my car and driving back to Portland?" Her voice rose as she spoke, edged with hysteria.

The gnome made a shushing noise and froze. With a growl, the dragon pounced, body changing as he moved through the air until it enlarged to the size of a small pony, the missing wing flowing up and out of the stub and the chips becoming whole. The dragon gleamed with smooth muscles under black scales lined with fire, hissing out a cloud of steam when it landed. A small dark shape under its paw chittered and flailed, but was securely hooked by the three-inch talons. In the light generated from the dragon's scales they could see a ragged shape looking like a piece of worn blanket, except it was transparent and wispy, the edges moving and reshaping. It suddenly leaped at her, attenuating from where the dragon secured it into a long thin shape snapping toward her face. The dragon slapped the tentacle down with his other paw causing it to narrowly miss her. The chittering noise became a high thin scream as the dragon played flame out of his nostrils across the black tattered shadow, carefully catching all the stray bits until only singed deck boards remained.

Sal wrapped her arms around herself and huddled in her chair. The deck smelled of burnt wood and the subtle decay she'd encountered in her Mom's bedroom. Nausea churned in her stomach and she felt the bite of acid in her throat. Tears blurred her world, and she reached blindly for the handful of tissues she'd stuffed into her skirt pocket earlier. The gnome was trying to comfort her with little pats to her back, probably bruising her, but she didn't care.

"Come on, you need to toughen up there. Crying isn't going to help," said the dragon. A figure crouched before her, not the dragon, but a man. Sal wondered where he'd come from but was too numb to react. Exerting effort, she controlled her tears and blew her nose. She didn't believe anything else could shock her but when she could see the man squatting before her clearly, her mind stuttered.

After Dad had died, Mom had two things that gave her comfort. One was her yard sales and antiquing. The other was Clint

Eastwood movies.

In front of her, slowly unwinding his lanky body to his feet, was the iconic actor from his days in spaghetti westerns. Piercing eyes squinting at her as if looking through a desert sun. Leonine hair brushed back from a tanned forehead. A thin black cigar clenched in straight white teeth between snarling lips. Spurs clinked when he moved, the fringed serape just as she remembered.

He removed the cigar, spat a bit of tobacco on the deck and said, "My name is Firewind, but you can call me Clint."

CHAPTER 6

Sally woke with a pain in her ribs. She shifted and reached under her side, removing a wad of tissues, hardened into the size of a baseball from use. Eyes still closed, she breathed deeply, remembering the funeral, so glad it was behind her. She didn't remember falling asleep on the couch last night but she must have woken up and crawled under the throw at some point. She felt peaceful and took another couple of deep breaths through her nose, pathetically glad the pain was muted, at least for now. She hugged the thought of meeting Mom in her dreams and saying a last goodbye. *But the other weird dream! Gnomes?* She smiled to herself, remembering. *It seemed so real.*

Yawning she stretched, arching her back and neck until bones creaked then opened her eyes.

A man's face hovered before her own. Sal shrieked and jumped up, scrambling over the back of the couch. She was panting in reaction, reality swamping her. She *had* talked to a gnome and a little stone dragon. The dragon had morphed into a bigger, real dragon and then…

"I'm hungry." Youngish Clint stood, staring at her with piercing grey eyes, crinkled skin radiating from the outer corners. The scruff on his face showed dark against his tanned skin. He looked irritated when she didn't respond and spoke again.

"I have been waiting for you to regain awareness. I need fuel for this body if I am to be strong enough to protect you."

Sal tried to speak, but only managed a whimper.

Clint frowned and Sally realized the black cigar was missing. *Maybe he ate it?* She thought. He was still dressed like the man with no name from spaghetti western days, complete with spurs clinking when he shifted his weight. Sal moistened her mouth and swallowed then tried again.

“Don’t scare me like that. It’s not—not nice.”

Clint’s frown intensified and a hint of a sulk appeared. A rim of red light flared briefly around the edges of his grey eyes but was gone so quickly, she wasn’t positive she’d seen it.

Light streamed in the windows, its presence a warm hand on her face. A glance at the cat clock informed her it was almost noon. She hadn’t eaten much for days and only a little in the morning on the day of the funeral. *Only yesterday?* Hunger pinched at her stomach and she was suddenly ravenous.

.I’ll make breakfast,” she said.

Sally stood in front of the stove, watching eggs overcook with unseeing eyes, reliving her moonlight adventure. A long arm snaked around her and grabbed the fry pan. She shifted out of the way, then turned off the burner.

I cannot believe HE is in the kitchen.

She’d slept in her clothes and her suit skirt and blouse were hopelessly rumpled under the vintage frilled apron she’d found behind the kitchen door. The pancakes were smoking in the other pan and she quickly flipped them over. They were only singed a little. She added them to the growing stack on the warm plate in the oven and decided it was enough. She wasn’t sure how much ‘fuel’ her bodyguard needed, but suspected it would be more than was considered normal from the pound of bacon he had already consumed. The six eggs in the fry pan he’d snagged were rapidly disappearing when she placed the platter of pancakes and jug of maple syrup on the table. He reached over to drag the platter in front of him and she slapped his fingers. His hand was warm and looked like a regular human’s but the skin felt stiffer, as if a layer of armor hid beneath it. “Some of those are for me,” she said firmly.

He growled at her and tugged at the platter. The dish flipped and pancakes flew through the air. She grabbed a couple in reflex then sat, placing them on her plate and pouring syrup over them.

Clint surveyed the scatted food then scooped them up off his lap, shirt and table top, dumped them back on the platter then mimicked her by adding syrup. Ignoring his fork, he folded a pancake and took a big bite. A euphoric expression crossed his face and she saw him smile for the first time. A wholehearted pleasure was there, inconsistent with the cynical persona he had assumed. She smiled back in reflex until he grabbed the jug and started to gulp the contents. Shining strands of thick maple syrup escaped the sides of his mouth and oozed down his chin. When he finished, he wiped his face off and carefully licked the back of his hand clean. He hefted the jug at her asking eagerly, “Is there more?”

***

She wouldn’t let him eat the pancakes scattered across the floor, starting another batch while she fixed fake maple syrup with water, sugar and maple flavoring in the microwave.

His hovering was annoying. When Sal bumped into him the second time she stabbed a finger at the table and barked, “Sit.” She hid her surprise when he obeyed. Removing the last pancake from the pan Sal joined him at the table. Placing a heaping plate in front of him, she poured half of the hot syrup over it. She set the syrup pitcher on a trivet but he snatched it up and started to chug the contents.

She watched, horrified, as he chugged the scalding hot syrup as if it were cool water.

Finished, he gave a belch, releasing a little puff of smoke and started to shovel in the pancakes with his fingers, using them to chase every drop of syrup on the plate. With a groan of pleasure, he pushed back from the table and stood. His face looked content and the red rim of light was back in his eyes and remained this time.

“I haven’t felt this good in centuries! Thank you for the maple drink! I did not know such existed.” He paused and then added, “The first stuff was much better, much stronger than the second.”

How could he not have encountered syrup before?

She was framing her questions when there came a noise from the living room. "Hello? Anyone home?" The front door must have been unlocked because the neighbor, Mrs. Dawson, entered the breakfast nook from the front room, tailed by Mrs. Mendez, the little white haired general who had organized the gathering after the funeral.

Their genteel nosiness changed to shock. Sal felt her own heart racing and her eyes flicked between the women and Clint, as he posed hipshot behind the small table heaped with dirty dishes, in all his western costumed glory. She opened her mouth, not knowing what she was going to say.

"Hi ladies. What a beautiful morning. Have you met my cousin, Clint?"

"Is that—is that?" Mrs Mendez's voice squealed with excitement and shock. Mrs. Dawson simply stood dumb, gazing at Clint with amazed adulation.

"Oh, no, of course not. He's an—an impersonator. He had an all-night gig in the area and stopped by. Isn't the makeup amazing?" Sal knew she was babbling, but didn't think her audience noticed.

"Oh, of course, an impersonator," said Mrs. Mendez. "But he is so much like him! How wonderful!" The little old lady clapped her hands and beamed.

"Well, yes, it helps he looks so much like the original, only younger. Mom told you we were distantly related to the original, didn't she? Clint here was even named after him."

"Why no! She never said a word." Mrs. Dawson stepped up to the pseudo Clint and grabbed one of his sticky hands, shaking it vigorously while her words tumbled out. "I can't believe she hasn't mentioned . . ." She abruptly remembered Sunny Anderson was gone, buried just the day before and muted her excitement.

Just then Sal's cell phone filled the room with "Addicted to Love" at full volume. Sal snatched it up but not before the ladies and Clint got an eyeful of the professional headshot Eric used for his contacts.

"Excuse me," she mumbled and rushed from the room.

"Hello, Eric, I'm so glad you called." Sal could hear the shakiness in her voice as she gushed into her phone.

Eric cut over her voice unceremoniously. "When are you returning? Have you found a Realtor and listed the house yet?"

"No, not yet, I haven't decided what I'm going to do." Sally's voice calmed even as she felt her insides freeze up. The pain she had struggled with for almost a week came back full force and she thought her knees would have buckled if she hadn't sat down on her mom's bed.

"Don't be ridiculous. Why would you keep a home you've never lived in? Hopefully your mother has some equity and you realize some real money from it. Do you have an appraisal yet?"

Sal spoke from her tightening throat, "Aren't you going to ask me about the funeral? Or ask me how I'm doing?"

His voice was cold. "I'm not a sentimental person, as you know. I hardly knew your mother."

"But you know me," she said softly and ended the call. Tears blurred her vision while she opened Eric's contact info and blocked his number. She hesitated for a moment, finger poised to unblock. *He will be so angry with me.* Sal blanked the screen instead and slid her cell into her pocket.

When she returned to the kitchen, both ladies were crowding Clint. They fawned over him and patted his arm fondly although the little white haired woman spared a moment to run a critical eye over the mess in the kitchen. Sal was wondering how she was going to get rid of them when the doorbell rang, followed by a brisk knock.

Clint skirted the women and was beside Sally before she took a step. “Let me check this out first,” he growled and went to the door, jerking it open while she followed close behind.

A large package with a smaller one teetering on top rested on the front porch next to the door. A cheerful horn toot called their attention to the FedEx truck zipping away from the curb. Clint bent and lifted the two packages easily, shutting the door with his foot. Sal and the two older women trailed him back into the kitchen where Sal hurriedly cleared a space on the table so he could put them down.

“Looks like you got something, Deary.” Mrs. Mendez eyed the packages, craning her neck to look at the labels.

Before Sal could respond, the doorbell rang again. Clint strode back to the front door, trailed by the women and opened it to a tall skinny man in brown shorts and shirt. “I got a delivery for Ms. Anderson. Need a signature.”

“I’m her daughter.” Pushing Clint aside so she could reach the door, Sal took the electronic clipboard and signed her name.

“I’m going to have to use the jack to move it, it ain’t coming up these stairs.” The UPS man jerked his head toward a large wooden crate resting on a pallet jack at the bottom of the ramp from his truck.

Sal grabbed Clint’s arm before he could move, picturing him picking up the heavy crate and carrying it into the house as if it were cardboard while they all goggled. *Not going to happen.*”

The garage, I’ll open the garage door if you’ll bring it in,” she said to the UPS man.

Mom always parked her Buick on the curb. The garage hugging the street was full of stuff, even more than the house, although most was boxed up. Sally thought there might be enough room if she shoved and stacked to fit the crate in.

The UPS truck drove away and they returned to the front room, closing and locking the door behind them. Sal realized the two older ladies weren't there and hoped they'd gone home but the sound of staples popping out of cardboard told her where they were.

When she entered the kitchen she found them removing gnomes and other lawn ornaments in various sizes and condition from the two boxes, tisk-ing over the frivolous purchase. Among the many male gnomes, there was a sturdy girl gnome, a jockey, and a small gargoyle.

"Oh, he's so cute!" Mrs. Mendez cradled the little gargoyle in her arms with difficulty. It was obviously a heavy piece, even with its small size—probably solid marble.

"Could I have him? As a memento of your mother?"

Sal realized her jaw had dropped and snapped it shut. This was embarrassing. Giving her the small statue would be the right gesture, but it had to stay so it *(he? she?)* could escape in two nights.

"I'm sorry, but I'm not supposed to give anything away until the estate is settled," she blurted, knowing the excuse was feeble, but unable to come up with anything else.

The older lady's face froze and she dropped the small statue to the table with a thunk. "I think we should leave, Eleanor," she said and marched out of the room.

With a disapproving look, Mrs. Dawson followed, leaving a wilting Sal alone in the kitchen with Clint. They heard the door slam and Clint left the room briefly, probably to make sure they had left and to lock the front door once more. Sal sank to the table and rested her face in her hands, shading her eyes.

"What's wrong?"

Sal dropped her hands. "I mortally offended my Mom's friends, that's what's wrong. At least we have more of your people though."

"A few more," Clint agreed. "But why didn't you let her have the gargoyle?"

"Isn't it one of you?"

He gave a gritty Clint laugh and nodded toward it scornfully. "That? It's not even a shell. Just a small statue, poorly made. I thought it ungracious of you not to gift it to the old lady."

He gently hoisted several of the gnomes and the small jockey in his arms and carried them out into the back yard.

CHAPTER 7

It was the evening of the full moon. Following Clint's directions, they'd combed the small city, buying gnomes and other yard ornaments from second hand stores, flea markets and yard sales. The statuettes never moved or spoke, but still gave her the creeps. Some of his people were scattered across front and back yards in the city and suburbs. Clint spent hours after dark retrieving them. *Okay, stealing them.* Through the kitchen windows she could see the beds surrounding the lawn were thickly clustered with yard gnomes sprinkled with a few other types of figures. There were no dragons, though, none she could see. She hadn't been able to go outside into the yard with them there. A few had been in the front, for protection Clint said; she walked by them quickly, averting her eyes.

Sal thought of Eric, wishing she knew if he'd tried to call, but something kept her from unblocking his number. She would deal with him and their relationship when it was all over. She'd made a Costco run and purchased a case of pure maple syrup. Clint had drunk most of it. He didn't look so much like a young version of the actor now. He seemed bigger, a little taller and beefier and almost shimmered with power. At her request, he had grown, in minutes, a full, dark brown beard to hide his features. His hair was covered by a billed cap. Stripped down to jeans, shirt and boots with an old wool plaid shirt as a jacket, he resembled the locals closely enough. The cap and shirt were her dad's; she had cried a little over them when she'd found in her mom's closet.

Clint was away, doing a last scan of the city and surrounding suburbs, hoping to sense a few more of his people. The doorbell rang and she answered before remembering she wasn't supposed to while Clint was away.

She relaxed when she saw the same tall and skinny UPS guy from a couple of days before.

He gave her a toothy grin along with the electronic

clipboard and said, “Nice evening. Got another package for you, not so big this time.” He held out a large quilted envelop and she took it automatically. The gnomes they set to guard the front of the house had been moved to the back for the night’s full moon. When the tingle ran up her arm, she knew something was wrong. The man smiled again, this time with an edge of nasty. She jerked away and slammed the door in his face, locking the dead bolt. Rasping laughter filtered through the heavy wood and she shuddered. Sal shuddered again when she realized her hand still griped the envelope, refusing to respond when she tried to drop it.

The tingling turned to pain slowly flowing up her arm. She trembled, afraid of what would happen when it reached her body

***

Clint drove the old Buick up to the curb and sat there, taking deep breaths. It was efficient transportation since he couldn’t use his wings and even fun when he went fast with the windows down so he could sample the scents on the wind. He’d even had fun playing with humans in another vehicle, one with bright lights and a loud voice. He supposed he should have stopped sooner, he recognized them from the Clint movies. Sally had warned him against driving fast when she demonstrated the car. When he slowed and pulled to the side of the road, two men in dark police uniforms advanced cautiously. A quick nudge of his mind blurred theirs’ and they returned to their vehicle, convinced he was a fellow law officer. It was the only fun he’d had. His last circuit had been a waste of time and his head hurt from straining at the limits of his senses for hours. He needed more maple syrup.

Halfway to the little house he stopped, as if he’d walked into an invisible wall. An aura of darkness swirled over him, coming from the house. Running to the door and he pounded on it, but Sal didn’t respond. His head jerked around at the sound of breaking stone from the back yard. Leaping off the porch, he race around the house, not pausing fothe gate, jumping easily over the six foot cedar fence.

Clint landed on all fours, morphing into his true shape although he kept it small to conserve power. He felt a tug of grief as he changed. He had used his power drunkenly over the last few days, easily regenerating it afterward with the maple syrup. Sal had helped him try the syrup with the others, but in their stone forms, they were unable to absorb it, and their powers were too depleted to allow them to change. *Would he be able to change back to the Clint form?* It didn't matter. He must fight, depleting his powers if necessary.

The back yard was shadowed in twilight. The moon was hours from rising and the porch was dark. He sensed movement and saw Sal walk out of the darkness under the trees lining the fence across the yard. He would have called out but something was wrong.

Sally reached one of the gnomes, and raised something hidden at her side. With a grunt of effort, she lifted a sledge hammer above her head with two hands and struck the gnome. A chunk of stone went flying as a thin shriek wailed across the grass.

She raised it again, preparing to strike. He didn't realize he was moving until he knocked her over. She tumbled, somehow retaining her hold on the sledge hammer and used the momentum of her fall to strike at him. The head of the hammer bounced off his scales with abnormal force. It was his turn to tumble. He lay on the torn up grass stunned and watched Sal rise to her feet. Some blood trickled down the side of her head and she limped as she approached him. A fixed grin, a rictus, distorted her face and he saw blackness engulfed her eyes. Sal was gone. Evil rode her, was going to kill Clint and all of his people gathered there.

He was helpless, unable to move although he could feel his muscles slowly knitting together. He could still stop her though, with a breath. Clint gathered the fires in his belly, building them into the heat living in the bowels of the earth. It would incinerate her instantly, this human. This human had talked with him, worked with him for his people, had become his friend. Agony twisted him inside, but he grimly continued to build his flame.

He would make it as quick as he could.

She was before him, raising the hammer easily now. The blackness shone greasily from her eyes.

He opened his mouth to flame, but spoke instead.

"Sal, don't do this. Fight it." The desperation in his voice shamed him. *Why do I hesitate to do what is necessary?*

The figure above him paused. Eyes blinking, he could see her sway, sledge hammer

upraised. His fire was at peak, a burst of flame and she would flash to dust. The corruption filling her would take a little longer, but it would have no host and would be impotent against the gnomes and dragon until he had recovered enough to find and destroy it. But Sal would be gone.

Still she stood above him. *Was there a hint of blue within the black? Is she fighting the evil invader?* His duty was clear but he couldn't do it. There must be some way to save her.

He remembered her mother and his effort to draw the blackness from her the night she died. *Had the plan been for Sunny to be possessed as her daughter now was—to destroy the gnomes?* The darkness had stopped Sunny's heart before he could draw it out of her. Yet he was much more powerful now and in his true dragon form. Even as the thought crossed his mind, he saw the thinning film boil across Sal's eyes until they were black holes absorbing all hope and light. The hammer descended with lightning speed but he twisted away. The blow shook the ground like a small earthquake, burying the head in the earth half the way up the handle. The creature controlling Sal pulled it free, whipping it up for another blow. He opened his mouth and sucked in breath instead of releasing it. He drew and drew using every bit of power he had left. *Was the blackness thinning?*

The creature controlling Sal dropped the hammer and slapped hands over its eyes. Still he drew in until he saw thin treads of black leaching between its fingers. He renewed his efforts and felt the foulness enter his mouth. It flashed to nothingness as it entered the furnace of his gullet. A scream escaped Sal's lips, full of agony and hate. He continued to draw and the figure dropped to its knees before him. But now his breath faltered. He, a dragon, was running out of breath, unable to continue as his power diminished. He could feel himself shrinking in size. He turned his head and puffed out a breath, releasing supper heated air capable of destroying Sal's body instantly. As he turned aside, he felt the gnomes surrounding him, ringing him with power. Turning back, Sal's form still knelt before him, its hands dropped to its sides.

Patches of black coursed over her pupils, revealing bits of blue and white. The manic smile was gone and her face was drawn in lines of fatigue and stress.

"We thought none of you could change anymore. It has been centuries since one of you changed into flesh." The being spoke with Sal's voice but the bitterness and malice had never come from her.

"Release her and I will let you go free." He felt the silent protest of the gnomes, but ignored it.

A manic laugh ratcheted from it, echoing off the fence surrounding the back yard.

"I, release her? I shall keep her and you will submit! If you resist, I shall kill her as her mother was killed." The being laughed again and reached claw-like hands toward him.

"So you feel lucky?" Clint growled. *I will have to do it,* he thought and dredged the last of his power together in a breath. He felt himself stiffen as he poured power into this last moment, this last betrayal of his friend.

The hands reaching for him stopped and then the figure

bent, one hand thrust into its mouth. It convulsed and hissed, then blackness vomited from its lips, along with Sal's lunch.

It continued to heave for several moments but nothing more came forth. She settled back on her heels swaying weakly. He looked into eyes as clear as pooled water then flamed the mess of blackness to ash.

CHAPTER 8

The gnomes and other yard ornaments seemed to fill the back yard with their presence. The broken remnants near the house scattered in the flower beds and at the foot of the trees were dimly visible in the light of the just risen moon. The relief of surviving, of being cleansed of the foulness that had controlled her body, was being eroded by the memories of what she had done. She remembered the dark pleasure as she pounded gnomes into shards of rock, absorbing their essence like a fine meal. Yet the essence had not been incorporated into the darkness. It had burned within her and encased her with a bubble of light. She had broken her bonds briefly, enough to stop the killing blow. When the dragon started to draw out her invader, Sal had mustered her will again, pushing the blackness away with everything she had. Clint had collapsed and when the creature taunted him, and she found the strength to finish expelling it, pushing with her will and the light, encasing it, then thrusting her fingers down her throat and vomiting it out.

"Are you well?" The squeaky voice of Oakheart came from near her feet and she looked down at him.

"I think so. What happens now?"

"The moon is full and *now* is the time to create the gate. Our people are fading and we will never be as strong, or the Enemy as weak as at this moment."

"I'm so sorry for what I did." Sal felt tears dribbling down her cheeks and wiped them away. She was so tired, tired of grief and fear.

"You were taken," the old gnome said, patting her awkwardly on the knee. "You helped us, knowingly, in spite of the danger. It is we who are in your debt, you and your mother."

Something stirred behind her and she spooked, turning swiftly. It was Clint. He creaked when he moved, and he seemed curiously shrunken. Shocked, she realized he was the size of a large dog rather than a pony and his scales were dull, only a flicker of light sparking occasionally on the tips. She dropped to her knees sitting back on her heels and he sank to the ground, allowing his head to rest in her lap, it was so heavy it was painful."What's wrong?" she cried, and circled his head in her arms.

"He is almost depleted," squeaked the gnome beside them.

"I'll get him some syrup," she said and pushed at his head but it didn't move. "I fear it is too late," rumbled the voice of the dragon.

"Nonsense, we have to try." She forced his head off her lap, ignoring the scales cutting through her jeans into the flesh beneath.

***

She moved as quickly as she could, limping out of the house cradling the last three jugs of syrup in her arms. The yard was bathed in the moonlight as it had been the night she had first met the gnome and Clint. The light was even more beautiful, etching the scene in her memory in grays and silver. The gnomes and other ornaments radiated from the center of the lawn, a clear space where only Oakheart and Clint remained. Oakheart was a solid presence, rooted into the ground and towering into the air with invisible force. Clint sprawled a short distance away, somehow not part of the circle or the center. He no longer crouched on his paws. He was on his belly, legs splayed, wings drooping around him instead of being folded against his sides. He looked pale in the moonlight and there were no more flickers of light along the edges of his scales.

Sal hurried, limping unsteadily through the gnomes until she reached the center. Clint's eyes were half closed and his tongue was protruding from his mouth. Her breath hitched, then a thin puff of smoke escaped his nostrils. *He is still alive!* She unscrewed the lid and then ripped the seal off the top of one of the jugs. Sticky syrup splashed over her hands. Ignoring it she poured syrup on the dragon's tongue. It lay there a moment before wisping away as steam. Clint didn't stir. She poured on more, drenching his head with it. Some steamed away but most of the syrup remained. *Was that good or bad?*

Around her the air seemed to pulse with sound just outside of her range of hearing. She emptied the jug and this time it remained, puddling in the grooves of his hide. The syrup started to glow and she felt hope then realized it was reflected light.

Turning, she was stunned, the jugs tumbling from her hand she dropped to the ground, legs too weak to hold her.

It was Oakheart, yet it wasn't. Instead of a comical figure, he had changed, becoming a creature crouching on muscular hind legs, great wings arched above him. The stone gnome had disappeared and a living gargoyle remained, limbs outlined in moonlight. Talons tipped his hands and feet, and great fangs splayed from his mouth. She should have been frightened, and deep down she probably was. Only the eyes were kind and gentle. Large and dark and lovely, soothing her with their light.

Then his jaws opened. And opened. Wider and wider they stretched. First his face disappeared, then his body, until only the open mouth and wide splaying jaws were visible. Light bloomed in the opening, a spiraling ball of all colors containing no color. She thought there was a sound, but strain as she might, it was snatched away and she realized all the night sounds surrounding her moments before were gone. But were they? Then the green smell of the grass, the pungent needles of the firs were gone, along with every other scent. Yet all these and more seemed to hover just out of reach. Did she feel something against her cheek? But no, she felt nothing, her body floated in nothing. Flavors bloomed in her mouth and then were gone and she couldn't remember how a strawberry tasted.

The light grew and grew, drawing the moon from the sky in bands of silver. She saw light flowing from the gnomes encircling them, from all but Clint and she knew he was no more. The wonder of the moment was broken by sorrow, and then the sorrow was gone too. She floated and wanted nothing but to be swallowed by the light.

Time stopped and she contemplated the universe and stars whose light was also being drawn down until strings of starlight encased the circle. There was a last pulse and then darkness. Oakheart's jaws still stretched wide and the circle of light had vanished, becoming heat, and warmth and life. The moonlight returned, but its magic was gone. She drew in a breath and yearned for the life she felt evolving on the other side. Her hands lifted of their own volition, reaching out to the life filling the gate. She could feel a rich surge of growth and images filled her mind of robust, rampant activity and change and then her thoughts were pulled away too. Even as she reached for it, the gate stilled. In the stillness she heard a voice in her head, triumphant. "Come, I am the gate and we have are a new world."

She couldn't move, couldn't look away but saw from the corner of her eyes, the stone gnomes wisp into dust, first those by the gate, then those farther away in a widening circle. Horror filled her and then she realized the gate was drawing in the essence of each of the gnomes as their bodies were destroyed, like the light she had absorbed during her rampage. The process seemed an eternity encased in a moment. She felt the light within her pulling loose and Sal struggled to follow. The forces entering the gate coalesced into an unimaginably small pinpoint and then flashed into immensity. Fresh new life, a new universe existed beyond the gate. She sensed pieces of herself but also a gulf of utter strangeness. She found herself kneeling, empty, before the gate and then it closed.

The grief almost broke her. Sally's memories of the world within the gate clouded almost at once, leaving hints nearly shattering her will, but obscuring enough to allow bearing her loss. She wasn't alone. Clint's body lay beside her and Oakheart, in his gargoyle shape was crouched in the center of the lawn. The moon dipped toward the trees, still bathing the grass with light. They were gone. All the gnomes they had collected were dust dancing in the breeze.

When Sal tried to stand, her body protested, cramped from remaining in one position so long. Mechanically she rubbed at her thighs and calves until they tingled with returning feeling. She lurched a little when she rose, almost tripping over Clint's body. The tears came and she was helpless to stop them. Drops dripped from her chin, falling on Clint, mixing with the syrup coating his head. She was crying for her mom, for Clint and for a new world, fresh with promise beyond her reach.

"There child, don't cry so. 'Twas not meant for you or me."

Still blubbering, she turned to Oakheart, "Why not? Why didn't you go too?"

"I am the gate. All I was and all I could be went into the gate except a small part meant to remain.

"Why didn't you let me enter?"

"It was not your fate, although I fear you have given up some of yourself too," said Oakheart, sadness echoing in his voice. "You are young and will heal. My people were ready to lay down their burdens and become something new. They are no more."

"I don't understand," said Sal.

With a groan, Oakheart settled back on his haunches. "We didn't go to a new world, we created a new world a new universe, but in so doing, we had to sacrifice all we were." His leathery skin was loosing its gleam.

Sniffing, she blew her nose into a used tissue she'd dug out of her jean pocket until it was sodden and dropped it on the grass. "I wish, even if I couldn't go, Clint could have survived to be part of it."

Oakheart cocked his head, his beautiful eyes luminous as

the moon finally faded below the trees. "He was never meant to go either. He has been a fierce protector of humans and our folk for many years, yet never quite one of us. His mother was of our people, but his father…" Shaking his head, he sighed. "He was to be my guardian here, until our people were freed. I am weakened and am returning to stone. In time my essence will fade from the world."

"Wait!" Sal picked up a full jug of syrup and opened it, passing it to Oakheart. "Can you drink or absorb food as you are now?"

"Well, yes, but there is no need. We do not gain substance from food and drink, we gain energy from light."

"Can you change to human form?"

"None of us can, except the dragon." Curious, he dropped some of the liquid on his tongue. Nothing happened. Oakheart straightened, and poured the maple syrup down his throat. He was neater than Clint had been the first time and only a little syrup clung to his fangs and muzzle. His long tongue quickly cleaned his lips and jaw, but there was no eagerness to it. They waited but Oakheart's skin continued to dull and he seemed stiffer in his movements. Even his great eyes seemed to dim.

"It is no use child."

"You can't give up! Clint may be gone but you're still alive. You have to fight."

Oakheart straightened. "Maybe there's a chance. I could live many years while gradually fading away or I might be able to…" His voice trailed off thoughtfully.

Oakheart stretched out, the lawn cradling his creaking body. One clawed hand reached out and cupped the dragon's head. Light flared where Oakheart touched the dragon. Sal felt a moment of hope but the light quickly died, leaving them in the soft glow of pre-dawn. Oakheart stirred feebly.

“Goodbye girl,” he said and was still.

Sal looked down at them, two stone monsters who’d invaded her life, and then were torn from her. She stood over them, dry eyed, and weary. The tears might come again, but she didn’t think so. She was afraid those unshed tears would stay, bottled up inside her, capping off her emotions for the rest of her life.

Her legs collapsed under her, dropping her to the lawn beside her friends. She watched as Oakheart’s appearance changed, the change accelerating until he was a beautifully detailed statue of a gargoyle. Then cracks appeared and his skin started to crumble.

Moments later, sand trickled from the cracks until he was a pile of dust and stones, lying next to a stone dragon.

Sally bowed her head, covering her sore, tired eyes with her hands. When her cell vibrated in her pocket, she listlessly pulled it out and answered.

“Hello?”

“Sally, I’ve been trying to reach you! My calls are being blocked.” Eric’s voice sounded both impatient and accusing.

“Did you think it might have been a hint?” Sal felt nothing when she replied, not even the sarcasm implied by her words.

“So you’re going to pout now,” said Eric. “So typical. Just because I didn’t cater to your emotions, you think you can manipulate me with a cold shoulder.”

He paused but Sal was silent.

“Come back at once. I expect to see you later today.”

“Why?” Sal gently reached out and touched Oakheart’s remains. The dust felt soft under her fingers, like powdered sugar. She couldn’t look at Clint, afraid of what she would see.

“Why?” Eric’s voice was a scream. “We’re almost engaged.

Get hold of yourself and discard this childish fit. It will not work on me."

"Goodbye, Eric." She couldn't hear the words but he sounded furious before she cut the connection. For good measure, she blocked the new number he had called from then turned her phone off. She had broken up with Eric. She felt vaguely as if she'd scraped something nasty off her shoe rather than ended a relationship. Sal dropped her head into her hands again and rocked a little, trying to find some hope of comfort.

"That guy sounds like a real dick." The voice croaked brokenly and Clint stood before her, swaying on two legs, his face and body gaunt like he had starved himself for weeks.

Sal burst into tears then laughed as she cried, jumping up to hug him. She felt him enfold her in his arms for a long moment and rested her head against his shoulder, ignoring how her skin and hair stuck to the half dried syrup coating him. He released her, her clothes and skin making a sucking sound as she moved back. Sal looked up, smiling into those keen grey eyes. He leaned over and whispered, "Anymore of that magic syrup?"

The End

TERESA KELLY

entered the magic worlds of the books she read early—second grade! She became a voracious reader, to the point that her mother had to regulate her reading. Throughout her life, she carried a book with her—now a tablet—to take advantage of stolen moments to read. She was a storyteller before becoming a writer. She dreamed up tales that she and her childhood friends acted out, and is a daydreamer still. She started to journal as a teen but didn't seriously try to record her stories until her forties when she was invited to join a writing group at work. She still works out the basis of her stories in her head before putting them on paper.
She loves writing. Editing? Not so much.

ALL THE LIVES HE HAD EVER LIVED LED TO THIS SINGLE MOMENT ...

CRASH DIVE

WAYNE KYLE

SPITZER

AUTHOR OF *THE WITCH-DOCTOR* AND *THE FLASHBACK SAGA*

T-minus 15 and counting. All set there, Chief?

I look at my reflection in the cockpit's front window—the tired eyes, the premature wrinkles and crow's feet—and beyond: to the blue hole and return mirror—which will remain invisible to the naked eye until I am almost upon it.

Roger that. All systems are go and I am hot to drop.

Roger that, *Diver 7.* Nine and counting: 8 … 7 … 6 …

I brace myself as the launch indicator switches from red to green—like a streetlight in the void—and the helmet's blue visor lowers … locking into place.

2 … 1 …

I grip the Jesus handles.

Launch.

Elton John once sang, "And all this science, I don't understand. It's just my job five days a week." That's how it is when you're a Crash Diver: you don't need to understand blue holes or how they differ from wormholes and black holes or what a mobius mirror does—only that it *must* work, every time—because, at the end of the day, that isn't your job. Your job is to be a guinea pig: to be shot into the vortex at near light speed and experience what effect blue hole-assisted mirror travel has on the human body and psyche. Your job is to penetrate to whatever depth they've set the mirror—and, if you're lucky, to enter that mirror and get bounced back.

It hasn't always been like this. Before there was *Zebra Station*—with its luxurious gravity centrifuge and its row of black and yellow delta divers hanging like bats from the launch jib—there was *Blue One,* a sparsely-manned outpost which had sent the first human souls into the maw of the blue hole, men who had come back white-haired and emaciated, debilitated—mentally and physically—mad.

The Crash Diver Program changed all that. From now on only specially-trained pilots would be sent into the Hole, pilots who had the benefit of the first men's experiences as well as spacecraft designed specifically for the task. A lot was learned in a very short time—one of these things was that men who entered the vortex experienced a series of hallucinations, or Dive Visions, in which they briefly felt they had become someone or something else: a soldier in the Holy Roman Army, say, or a person of the opposite sex. Some even purported to have become animals or alien lifeforms—it was the latter which had apparently driven the men of *Blue One* clinically insane.

Another lesson was the fact that the farther a mirror was projected into the vortex the farther it could "cast" to its attendant portal; meaning the Hole might well hold the key to intergalactic space travel. This more than anything had accounted for the program's generous funding, not to mention its exhaustive launch table, which sometimes saw us drop as many as three times in a week. The chief problem, however, remained—and that was that the deeper one dropped, the more acute the hallucinations; hence, the missions had become increasingly volatile, increasingly dangerous.

Regardless, a decision had been made to make the next drop the deepest yet: all the way through the ergosphere—right up to the outer event horizon. By which they meant right up to the point of no return, even by mirror refraction.

And I was the one who drew the unlucky straw.

It is raining. That's the first thing I notice, the first thing that tells me I am no longer in the cockpit. The second is that I'm bleeding—bleeding from the leg, which is making it difficult to press the attack. The third is that I'm dying—as is my opponent—dying beneath a blood red sky.

"It is finished," he says, stumbling forward and back—his blood flowing freely, his hair matted in sweat. "Look at you! Your broadsword is shattered. Your armor is compromised. Why is it you continue?"

But I do not know why I continue—only that I was a Crash Diver once and will be so again, and so must face the vision, endure its consequences. Endure them so that future generations may bridge the gulf of galaxies!

At last I say: "Are you better off? We die together, Sir Aglovere. Surely you—"

But I am baffled by my own voice, so familiar and yet strange, and by my own words, which have materialized from nowhere.

And then he is charging, hacking at me wildly, and I am forced back along the hedgerow: until I lose my footing over a protruding root and topple headlong into the mud and bramble—whereupon my opponent falls on what's left of my sword and is promptly run through, his entrails unspooling like loops of linked sausage and his eyes turning to empty glass.

At length he says, "We kill ourselves," and laughs, even as I push him off me.

And then we just lay there, staring at the sky, neither of us saying anything, as our blood pools together and spirals down the slope. As the clouds continue to rumble—pouring rain into our dying eyes.

The diver trembles violently as I shake the vision off.

… repeat, *Zebra One* to Diver 7, are you all right?

I feel my leg through my flight suit, half expecting it to be flayed wide open—but I am unharmed, of course.

Roger that, *Zebra One.* However I am experiencing turbulence I cannot account for—what can you tell me?

There is a long pause which is pregnant with static, after which *Zebra One* responds, choppily, Diver 7 … *Zebra One.* Be advised … some kind of anomaly. We are working … before it effects the mirrors. Please …

And then they are gone.

I am gone, too. At least, I am no longer in the cockpit. Instead, I awaken from a dream I cannot remember in a place I have never been—no, I can see now that is incorrect. I am *home,* still sequestered in the dingy sleeping quarters at the very back of the Temple—where I have remained now for three days without benefit of food or water, and where I shall stay—unto death, if necessary—until Rue Umbra shows me His face. Until He Who Created Everything bestows upon me the gift of His Holy visage.

"Master Hezekiah … the Artifact is ready."

"Bring it to me, Jocasta. I will view it here in my chambers."

"Yes, Master."

I rise and swing my legs out of bed, and am startled briefly by my reflection in the bureau mirror. For it seems at first that I am someone—*something*—else; someone/something alien, with a gray, rumpled body and a face that is smooth like glass. Then it is gone and I see only myself: the green scales, the angled brow, the tired eyes of the High Priest of Samara.

At length Jocasta re-enters the room and places the box on the rug at my feet. "It is my hope—*our* hope, Master, the entire congregation's—that you will end your fast soon. May Rue Umbra light your way."

He moves to leave but hesitates, pausing in the doorway. "It is also hoped … that you will be careful. This so-called Artifact—it is not of this world."

Then he is gone and I am alone with the box, the box containing the meteor which has somehow survived its entry into our atmosphere. The hollow meteor with the strange runes printed on its surface (at least, that is how it has been described to me). The thing whose existence is responsible for my crisis of faith.

Show me, Oh Highest One. Send me a sign. Reveal to me, your faithful servant, the naked face of God.

But Rue Umbra is silent as I open the box and lift out the Artifact, and proceed to examine it by the dim light of the candles. Nor is the object so unfathomable as I'd presumed: for it is clearly something designed to protect the head, similar in many respects to our Centurions' helmets (although charred and blackened from its journey through the atmosphere) and composed of materials I have never seen; some of which glow at the touch of my fingers and cause the Artifact to hum and to vibrate …

Show me your face, Oh Lord, so that I may believe again!

But in the end there is nothing, only silence, as a glassy shield lowers smoothly and locks into place. As I stare into its curved, indigo-blue surface—which has become a kind of looking glass, a mirror—and see only myself, Hezekiah. Only the High Priest of Samara laid low by his fast.

Something is wrong. This much is clear as I stir from the vision and find the diver shaking—shaking as though it might fly apart any moment. *Zebra One,* meanwhile, is talking at me through my headset:

… get it back. We're trying … but … long shot. Repeat: we have … return mirror. It's just …

Again, damn you! You're breaking up. What about the mirror?

... has failed. We are trying—

But they are gone—and I am alone. Alone against the ergosphere, whose end must surely be near. Alone—in light of the mirror's failure—against the event horizon, beyond which lies Hell itself.

I pause, feeling it again. As though someone were in the cave with me, as though someone were watching.

I look to the mouth of the cavern, beyond which the snow continues to fall. No, it is nothing—the wind, perhaps, coursing through the opening.

I return to my work, continuing the stroke which will complete our leader (his snout blue with war paint, his shoulders broad and hairy), knowing he will be pleased. For I have captured him in truth—as well his shoulders broad and hairy), knowing he will be pleased. For I have captured him in truth—as well as the spirit of his hunt—captured him so that he might live for all time. And yet, as the winds moan and the torches falter, the feeling I am not alone persists, so that I again look to the door of the cave, and this time—someone is there.

The hominid doesn't move, doesn't seem to breathe, as I look at him, and for an instant I think, *Dr. Livingstone, I presume.* Then I laugh a little behind my visor, marveling that I can do so under the circumstances, and take a step forward, eliciting a growl from the creature I would not want to hear twice.

I hold, looking back at the diver—which is suspended nose-down in the middle of the air—before turning again to regard the creature and his art ... only to find them gone, replaced by a very old man in what appears to be a Tudor-style study parlor.

"Livingstone, Einstein, Hezekiah, we've been them all, at one time or another." He begins moving toward me, casually. "You are … Diver 7. I presume."

I just look at him, saying nothing. Behind him is a blackboard which runs floor to ceiling and wall to wall, and is crowded with equations. Noticing my gaze, he says, "Ah, yes. Well. The hominid has his work, and I have mine."

He stops within a few feet of me, examining my flight suit. "Your helmet. You won't be needing it."

I look at him for what seems a long time. At last I reach up and trigger the visor, which glides up and out of the way, and take a deep breath. The air is fine.

"Where am I?" I ask, glancing about the room, noting its exotic décor: a red, cactus-like plant (without needles) which looks as though it belongs at the bottom of an alien sea; a black and silver obelisk the height of a man; a polished suit of armor standing sentinel in a corner. "And who are you?"

The old man smiles, warmly, compassionately. "I should have thought you'd have guessed. As for where, why, you're stone cold dead in the middle of a blue hole. Where else? The mirrors, alas, have failed—but you knew that already. No, what you really want to know is … what does it all mean? The Hole, the visions, everything. Isn't that right, Diver 7?"

I look at the old man expectantly.

"Beats the hell out of me," he says, and moves toward the blackboard. "A blue hole is where mathematics go to die. No. What I have left is only conjecture, speculation—metaphysics rather than physics, notes as opposed to a complete script." He puts his hands on his hips, examining his formulas, and exhales, warily. "Of the trail of ink there is no end."

At length he begins moving again, pacing beyond the red plant and the black and silver obelisk, past the suit of armor which gleams like gold in the umber firelight. "Say, just say, for the sake of argument, that the Buddhists are right, and that reincarnation is real. And that its purpose is to evolve souls, to grow them—from the first spark of sentience to something approaching divinity. Would you allow that this was a worthy end to our travails?"

I don't say anything, only continue to watch him.

"Say, too, that these incarnations are infinite, or nearly so, occurring not just in this universe but a *multiverse,* so that, in time, we have experienced creation from every window and every door, every viewpoint—in short, we have been everyone and everything. *Mmm?* Shall we say it?"

He stops and turns around, begins pacing back toward me. "And that, as we reach the point of infinite progression, we begin to, slide, if you will, back and forth amongst our lifetimes—putting the lesson together, as it were, making of it a sphere, rather than a line, compressing everything into an infinitely dense mass, an Alpha and Omega, a singularity such as is found in the heart of our blue hole. Would you say then that we had solved the riddle of its phantasmagorias?"

He pauses not three feet away and I just look at him: the tired eyes, the deep wrinkles and crow's feet—at last, I understand.

I lift off my helmet.

"I was you, once," I say. "We were … We will …"

He nods, slowly. "Not only us but all men, all sentient beings. Nothing is wasted."

My mind reels. "But … The Hole. My diver. It took those things to—"

He laughs suddenly. "Oh, that. Why, that's just a happy coincidence. You still don't understand, do you? You never needed the ship, or the vortex. You—we—were ready. Our infinite progression had reached—"

"Madness," I say. "Shadows within shadows."

But he is gone, replaced by Hezekiah. "It's the shadows that exist," he says, and I understand him perfectly in spite of his alien tongue. "The objects that create them; those are the illusions. Put another way: The ghost is real—the machine is not. Now—it is time."

And I am back in the cave, standing so close to the hominid I can smell him, watching him rub chalk on the stone, watching him create entire worlds. Until he looks at me sidelong and hands me the tool—thoughtfully, knowingly—as if he were encouraging me. As if he were saying: *You too can do it. You, too, are the Creator.*

Until I close my fingers on the chalk and everything fades to black.

And that blackness becomes Light.

I am become the White Fountain, the creator of worlds—the Big Bang which will expand outward, creating a new universe. Nor has the previous universe ceased to exist; for it dreams behind us on the other side of the Hole—its galaxies and star systems safely intact, its sentience growing by leaps and bounds.

Meanwhile, even amidst the crash and swirl of creation, I have remained—the godhead of an entirely new paradigm; the observer, and yet, somehow, the observed; the ghost in the rapidly expanding machine. Nor has every vestige of my former self been annihilated; for something has survived the explosion which even now hurtles outward into the maelstrom, spinning, tumbling, drifting ever further. For a billion years, it drifts, until, caught by a mid-size world's gravitational pull, it falls like a shooting star into an alien sea—a sea as red as blood—whereupon, again, it *drifts.*

Until it is retrieved from the water by a pair of eager hands—four-fingered hands—which grip the helmet firmly and place it into the boat, after which it is passed from one being to the other like the physical manifestation of a riddle, and finally put into a box.

Where it will remain—its secrets safe, its numeral '07' unseen—until delivered to the priest.

The End

WAYNE KYLE SPITZER

is an American author and low-budget horror filmmaker from Spokane, Washington. He is the writer/director of the short horror film, *Shadows in the Garden*, as well as the author of *Flashback*, a Sci-Fi/Horror novel published in 1993. Spitzer's non-genre writing has appeared in *subTerrain Magazine: Strong Words for a Polite Nation* and *Columbia: The Magazine of Northwest History*. His recent fiction includes *The Ferryman Pentalogy*, consisting of *Comes a Ferryman, The Tempter and the Taker, The Pierced Veil, Black Hole, White Fountain,* and *To the End of Ursathrax*, as well as *The X-Ray Rider* Trilogy and a screen adaptation of Algernon Blackwood's "*The Willows*."

Books By Wayne Kyle Spitzer

God's Tears

Worlds without number lands before time
Creations made by My hands
Worlds of green and brilliant blue
Worlds for all mankind

Ever leaving, never seeing
that which I have done
Ever seeking, never thinking
Worlds for all mankind

Worlds of green and brilliant blue
I made them just for you
Crystalline tears fall from My eyes
Spheres from tears, it's true

Behold my creations, made by these hands
imbued with My own DNA
Worlds without numbers, lands before time
time after time after time

M. Kari Barr

THIS, O Best Beloved, is another story of the High and Far-Off Times. In the very middle of those times was a Stickly-Prickly Hedgehog, and he lived on the banks of the turbid Amazon, eating shelly snails and things. And he had a friend, a Slow-Solid Tortoise, who lived on the banks of the turbid Amazon, eating green lettuces and things. And so that was all right, Best Beloved. Do you see?

But also, and at the same time, in those High and Far-Off Times, there was a Painted Jaguar, and he lived on the banks of the turbid Amazon too; and he ate everything that he could catch. When he could not catch deer or monkeys he would eat frogs and beetles; and when he could not catch frogs and beetles he went to his Mother Jaguar, and she told him how to eat hedgehogs and tortoises.

She said to him ever so many times, graciously waving her tail, 'My son, when you find a Hedgehog you must drop him into the water and then he will uncoil, and when you catch a Tortoise you must scoop him out of his shell with your paw.' And so that was all right, Best Beloved.

One beautiful night on the banks of the turbid Amazon, Painted Jaguar found Stickly-Prickly Hedgehog and Slow-Solid Tortoise sitting under the trunk of a fallen tree. They could not run away, and so Stickly-Prickly curled himself up into a ball, because he was a Hedgehog, and Slow-Solid Tortoise drew in his head and feet into his shell as far as they would go, because he was a Tortoise; and so that was all right, Best Beloved. Do you see?

'Now attend to me,' said Painted Jaguar, 'because this is very important. My mother said that when I meet a Hedgehog I am to drop[103] him into the water and then he will uncoil, and when I meet a Tortoise I am to scoop him out of his shell with my paw. Now which of you is Hedgehog and which is Tortoise? because to save my spots, I can't tell.'

'Are you sure of what your Mummy told you?' said Stickly-Prickly Hedgehog. 'Are you quite sure? Perhaps she said that when you uncoil a Tortoise you must shell him out of the water with a scoop, and when you paw a Hedgehog you must drop him on the shell.'

'Are you sure of what your Mummy told you?' said Slow-and-Solid Tortoise. 'Are you quite sure? Perhaps she said that when you water a Hedgehog you must drop him into your paw, and when you meet a Tortoise you must shell him till he uncoils.'

'I don't think it was at all like that,' said Painted Jaguar, but he felt a little puzzled; 'but, please, say it again more distinctly.'

'When you scoop water with your paw you uncoil it with a Hedgehog,' said Stickly-Prickly. 'Remember that, because it's important.'

'But,' said the Tortoise, 'when you paw your meat you drop it into a Tortoise with a scoop. Why can't you understand?'

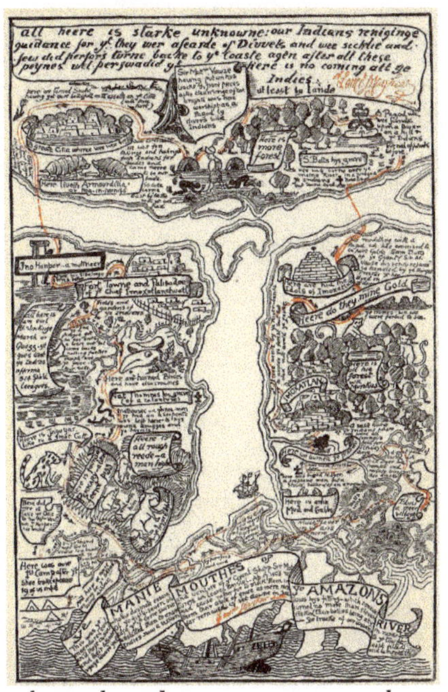

This is an inciting map of the Turbid Amazon done in Red and Black. It hasn't anything to do with the story except that there are two Armadillos in it—up by the top. The inciting part are the adventures that happened to the men who went along the road marked in red. I meant to draw Armadillos when I began the map, and I meant to draw manatees and spider-tailed monkeys and big snakes and lots of Jaguars, but it was more inciting to do the map and the venturesome adventures in red. You begin at the bottom left-hand corner and follow the little arrows all about, and then you come quite round again to where the adventuresome people went home in a ship called the Royal Tiger. This is a most adventuresome picture, and all the adventures are told about in writing, so you can be quite sure which is an adventure and which is a tree or a boat.

'You are making my spots ache,' said Painted Jaguar; 'and besides, I didn't want your advice at all. I only wanted to know which of you is Hedgehog and which is Tortoise.'

'I shan't tell you,' said Stickly-Prickly, 'but you can scoop me out of my shell if you like.'

'Aha!' said Painted Jaguar. 'Now I know you're Tortoise. You thought I wouldn't! Now I will.' Painted Jaguar darted out his paddy-paw just as Stickly-Prickly curled himself up, and of course Jaguar's paddy-paw was just filled with prickles. Worse than that, he knocked Stickly-Prickly away and away into the woods and the bushes, where it was too dark to find him. Then he put his paddy-paw into his mouth, and of course the prickles hurt him worse than ever. As soon as he could speak he said, 'Now I know he isn't Tortoise at all. But'—and then he scratched his head with his un-prickly paw— 'how do I know that this other is Tortoise?'

'But I am Tortoise,' said Slow-and-Solid. 'Your mother was quite right. She said that you were to scoop me out of my shell with your paw. Begin.'

'You didn't say she said that a minute ago,' said Painted Jaguar, sucking the prickles out of his paddy-paw. 'You said she said something quite different.'

'Well, suppose you say that I said that she said something quite different, I don't see that it makes any difference; because if she said what you said I said she said, it's just the same as if I said what she said she said. On the other hand, if you think she said that you were to uncoil me with a scoop, instead of pawing me into drops with a shell, I can't help that, can I?'

'But you said you wanted to be scooped out of your shell with my paw,' said Painted Jaguar.

'If you'll think again you'll find that I didn't say anything of the kind. I said that your mother said that you were to scoop me out of my shell,' said Slow-and-Solid.

'What will happen if I do?' said the Jaguar most sniffily and most cautious.

'I don't know, because I've never been scooped out of my shell before; but I tell you truly, if you want to see me swim away you've only got to drop me into the water.'

'I don't believe it,' said Painted Jaguar. 'You've mixed up all the things my mother told me to do with the things that you asked me whether I was sure that she didn't say, till I don't know whether I'm on my head or my painted tail; and now you come and tell me something I can understand, and it makes me more mixy than before. My mother told me that I was to drop one of you two into the water, and as you seem so anxious to be dropped I think you don't want to be dropped. So jump into the turbid Amazon and be quick about it.'

'I warn you that your Mummy won't be pleased. Don't tell her I didn't tell you,' said Slow-Solid.

'If you say another word about what my mother said—' the Jaguar answered, but he had not finished the sentence before Slow-and-Solid quietly dived into the turbid Amazon, swam under water for a long way, and came out on the bank where Stickly-Prickly was waiting for him.

'That was a very narrow escape,' said Stickly-Prickly. 'I don't like Painted Jaguar. What did you tell him that you were?'

'I told him truthfully that I was a truthful Tortoise, but he wouldn't believe it, and he made me jump into the river to see if I was, and I was, and he is surprised. Now he's gone to tell his Mummy. Listen to him!'

They could hear Painted Jaguar roaring up and down among the trees and the bushes by the side of the turbid Amazon, till his Mummy came.

'Son, son!' said his mother ever so many times, graciously waving her tail, 'what have you been doing that you shouldn't have done?'

'I tried to scoop something that said it wanted to be scooped out of its shell with my paw, and my paw is full of per-ickles,' said Painted Jaguar.

'Son, son!' said his mother ever so many times, graciously waving her tail, 'by the prickles in your paddy-paw I see that that must have been a Hedgehog. You should have dropped him into the water.'

'I did that to the other thing; and he said he was a Tortoise, and I didn't believe him, and it was quite true, and he has dived under the turbid Amazon, and he won't come up again, and I haven't anything at all to eat, and I think we had better find lodgings somewhere else. They are too clever on the turbid Amazon for poor me!'

'Son, son!' said his mother ever so many times, graciously waving her tail, 'now attend to me and remember what I say. A Hedgehog curls himself up into a ball and his prickles stick out every which way at once. By this you may know the Hedgehog.'

'I don't like this old lady one little bit,' said Stickly-Prickly, under the shadow of a large leaf. 'I wonder what else she knows?'

'A Tortoise can't curl himself up,' Mother Jaguar went on, ever so many times, graciously waving her tail. 'He only draws his head and legs into his shell. By this you may know the Tortoise.'

'I don't like this old lady at all—at all,' said Slow-and-Solid Tortoise. 'Even Painted Jaguar can't forget those directions. It's a great pity that you can't swim, Stickly-Prickly.'

'Don't talk to me,' said Stickly-Prickly. 'Just think how much better it would be if you could curl up. This is a mess! Listen to Painted Jaguar.'

Painted Jaguar was sitting on the banks of the turbid Amazon sucking prickles out of his paws and saying to himself—

'Can't curl, but can swim—
Slow-Solid, that's him!
Curls up, but can't swim—
Stickly-Prickly, that's him!'

'He'll never forget that this month of Sundays,' said Stickly-

Prickly. 'Hold up my chin, Slow-and-Solid. I'm going to try to learn to swim. It may be useful.'

'Excellent!' said Slow-and-Solid; and he held up Stickly-Prickly's chin, while Stickly-Prickly kicked in the waters of the turbid Amazon.

'You'll make a fine swimmer yet,' said Slow-and-Solid. 'Now, if you can unlace my back-plates a little, I'll see what I can do towards curling up. It may be useful.'

Stickly-Prickly helped to unlace Tortoise's back-plates, so that by twisting and straining Slow-and-Solid actually managed to curl up a tiddy wee bit.

'Excellent!' said Stickly-Prickly; 'but I shouldn't do any more just now. It's making you black in the face. Kindly lead me into the water once again and I'll practise that side-stroke which you say is so easy.' And so Stickly-Prickly practised, and Slow-Solid swam alongside.

'Excellent!' said Slow-and-Solid. 'A little more practice will make you a regular whale. Now, if I may trouble you to unlace my back and front plates two holes more, I'll try that fascinating bend that you say is so easy. Won't Painted Jaguar be surprised!'

'Excellent!' said Stickly-Prickly, all wet from the turbid Amazon. 'I declare, I shouldn't know you from one of my own family. Two holes, I think, you said? A little more expression, please, and don't grunt quite so much, or Painted Jaguar may hear us. When you've finished, I want to try that long dive which you say is so easy. Won't Painted Jaguar be surprised!'

And so Stickly-Prickly dived, and Slow-and-Solid dived alongside.

'Excellent!' said Slow-and-Solid. 'A leetle more attention

to holding your breath and you will be able to keep house at the bottom of the turbid Amazon. Now I'll try that exercise of wrapping my hind legs round my ears which you say is so peculiarly comfortable. Won't Painted Jaguar be surprised!'

'Excellent!' said Stickly-Prickly. 'But it's straining your back-plates a little. They are all overlapping now, instead of lying side by side.'

'Oh, that's the result of exercise,' said Slow-and-Solid. 'I've noticed that your prickles seem to be melting into one another, and that you're growing to look rather more like a pine-cone, and less like a chestnut-burr, than you used to.'

'Am I?' said Stickly-Prickly. 'That comes from my soaking in the water. Oh, won't Painted Jaguar be surprised!'

They went on with their exercises, each helping the other, till morning came; and when the sun was high they rested and dried themselves. Then they saw that they were both of them quite different from what they had been.

'Stickly-Prickly,' said Tortoise after breakfast, 'I am not what I was yesterday; but I think that I may yet amuse Painted Jaguar.'

'That was the very thing I was thinking just now,' said Stickly-Prickly. 'I think scales are a tremendous improvement on prickles—to say nothing of being able to swim. Oh, won't Painted Jaguar be surprised! Let's go and find him.'

By and by they found Painted Jaguar, still nursing his paddy-paw that had been hurt the night before. He was so astonished that he fell three times backward over his own painted tail without stopping.

'Good morning!' said Stickly-Prickly. 'And how is your

dear gracious Mummy this morning?'

'She is quite well, thank you,' said Painted Jaguar; 'but you must forgive me if I do not at this precise moment recall your name.'

'That's unkind of you,' said Stickly-Prickly, 'seeing that this time yesterday you tried to scoop me out of my shell with your paw.'

'But you hadn't any shell. It was all prickles,' said Painted Jaguar. 'I know it was. Just look at my paw!'

'You told me to drop into the turbid Amazon and be drowned,' said Slow-Solid. 'Why are you so rude and forgetful to-day?'

'Don't you remember what your mother told you?' said Stickly-Prickly,—

'Can't curl, but can swim—
Stickly-Prickly, that's him!
Curls up, but can't swim—
Slow-Solid, that's him!'

Then they both curled themselves up and rolled round and round Painted Jaguar till his eyes turned truly cart-wheels in his head.

Then he went to fetch his mother.

This is a picture of the whole story of the Jaguar and the Hedgehog and the Tortoise and the Armadillo all in a heap. It looks rather the same any way you turn it. The Tortoise is in the middle, learning how to bend, and that is why the shelly plates on his back are so spread apart. He is standing on the Hedgehog, who is waiting to learn how to swim. The Hedgehog is a Japanesy Hedgehog, because I couldn't find our own Hedgehogs in the garden when I wanted to draw them. (It was daytime, and they had gone to bed under the dahlias.) Speckly Jaguar is looking over the edge, with his paddy-paw carefully tied up by his mother, because he pricked himself scooping the Hedgehog. He is much surprised to see what the Tortoise is doing, and his paw is hurting him. The snouty thing with the little eye that Speckly Jaguar is trying to climb over is the Armadillo that the Tortoise and the Hedgehog are going to turn into when they have finished bending and swimming. It is all a magic picture, and that is one of the reasons why I haven't drawn the Jaguar's whiskers. The other reason was that he was so young that his whiskers had not grown. The Jaguar's pet name with his Mummy was Doffles.

'Mother,' he said, 'there are two new animals in the woods to-day, and the one that you said couldn't swim, swims, and the one that you said couldn't curl up, curls; and they've gone shares in their prickles, I think, because both of them are scaly all over, instead of one being smooth and the other very prickly; and, besides that, they are rolling round and round in circles, and I don't feel comfy.'

'Son, son!' said Mother Jaguar ever so many times,

graciously waving her tail, 'a Hedgehog is a Hedgehog, and can't be anything but a Hedgehog; and a Tortoise is a Tortoise, and can never be anything else.'

'But it isn't a Hedgehog, and it isn't a Tortoise. It's a little bit of both, and I don't know its proper name.'

'Nonsense!' said Mother Jaguar. 'Everything has its proper name. I should call it "Armadillo" till I found out the real one. And I should leave it alone.'

So Painted Jaguar did as he was told, especially about leaving them alone; but the curious thing is that from that day to this, O Best Beloved, no one on the banks of the turbid Amazon has ever called Stickly-Prickly and Slow-Solid anything except Armadillo. There are Hedgehogs and Tortoises in other places, of course (there are some in my garden); but the real old and clever kind, with their scales lying lippety-lappety one over the other, like pine-cone scales, that lived on the banks of the turbid Amazon in the High and Far-Off Days, are always called Armadillos, because they were so clever.

So that's all right, Best Beloved. Do you see?

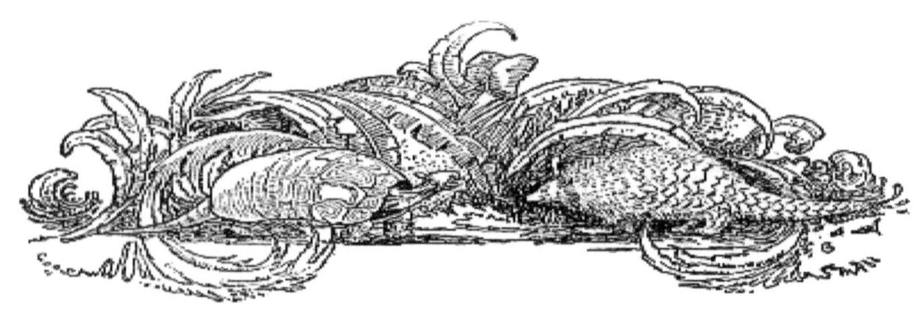

I've never sailed the Amazon,
I've never reached Brazil;
But the Don and Magdalena,
They can go there when they will!

Yes, weekly from Southampton,
Great steamers, white and gold,
Go rolling down to Rio
(Roll down—roll down to Rio!)
And I'd like to roll to Rio
Some day before I'm old!

I've never seen a Jaguar,
Nor yet an Armadill—
O dilloing in his armour,
And I s'pose I never will,

Unless I go to Rio
These wonders to behold—
Roll down—roll down to Rio—
Roll really down to Rio!
Oh, I'd love to roll to Rio
Some day before I'm old!

RUDYARD KIPLING

(30 December 1865 – 18 January 1936) is best known for *Jungle Book* published in 1894. But many have cherished his *Just So Stories* over the years as well. He was awarded the Nobel Prize in Literature in 1907, making him the first English-language writer to receive the prize.

He was recommended for the British Poet Laureateship and several times for a knighthood, but he declined both.

Kipling's father was an artist. A skill Kipling soon mastered as well. Raised in India until the age of 5, at which point he was sent to school in England, he was housed by a couple who treated him and his sister poorly. In his autobiography published 65 years later, Kipling recalled the stay with horror, and wondered if the combination of cruelty and neglect which he experienced might not have hastened the onset of his literary life: "If you cross-examine a child of seven or eight on his day's doings (specially when he wants to go to sleep) he will contradict himself very satisfactorily. If each contradiction be set down as a lie and retailed at breakfast, life is not easy. I have known a certain amount of bullying, but this was calculated torture — religious as well as scientific. Yet it made me give attention to the lies I soon found it necessary to tell: and this, I presume, is the foundation of literary effort."

Kipling was freed from his schooling there at age 11, and returned to India when he was 16. For him it was home; even when he returned to England, his early life and career never left his heart.

Begin
(a graphic poem)

Begin

Allegiance

Trinity

All My Religions

Making

Babel

New Worlds

The following pages are collages crafted by May Cotton. Each collage is entitled with the words of the poem above, making up the graphic poem.

Start something
DEEP
SCATTERED
Essential
wild
NO
fear
AFTER

Begin

Allegience

Trinity

All My Religions

Making

Babel

New Worlds

The Writings of Richard Lasater

A Poet's Heart

THE UNDERTOW

I know this place well,
oily sand, broken

tracks all over like long snakes
sent from Detroit City.

The ocean falls back while my sons watch
me watch for signs of undertow.

Breaking back, the fast stream
cuts the tide like a highway into a hill.

It does what waves should do,
run to us in crests of boiling snow.

I lead my trusting sons into this,
to the second trench between the sand bars.

The undertow, this ton of grabbing hands,
sucks us from shallow water.

My sons across my shoulders,
each face's ghost shows through,

until that moving mountain picks us up
like pebbles, throws us back, to sand.

Tonight I dream of drowning
faces covered with big eyes. They will
prowl forever.

— Richard Lasater

Originally published in *Amphora Review, The University of Texas El Paso Literary Magazine*, Vol. 2 No. 4, Dec. 4, 1981.

ADOBE ROAD

Freewaying acrosss New Mexico
you ease off the accelerator,
off the concrete four lane
onto highway 26, on a whim,
maybe nudged by some great grandfather's
ghost. You bridge the rusty Rio Grande,
drained like the dried up breasts
of an old woman. Your road cuts
between mountains chewed down
by sand storms to nothing
but bleached bone.

The Chihuahuan Desert sprawls
so far ahead it make the land
look strange when the yucca runs
to grass and cattle, going west.
Three pickups lounge outside
the bar that sprang up from thirst
and loneliness eighty miles this side
of Silver City where the Hillsboro
sign says thirty-one. The land is climbing
now and to the west adobe walls come up
from nothing. You've been seeing
them for centuries. They were little
forts against the sand and sun
back when the river had no fear.

Summer shimmers wave the air,
wave you from your air conditioned Audi
into screaming August insects,
across an arroyo with cirrhosis of erosion,
past a spiny Blunt-nosed Leopard Lizard,
to where July Navajo male rain storms
have stormed this adobe ruin.
Straw sticks out from melting bricks
like six day whiskers
on a burned out man.

Tumbleweeds crawl each other, pile
past the window some brown child gazed
through at stars he'd never reach.
Sunlight catches on an orange spider's web
hanging broken as a peon
family's blistered dreams.
You hold your breath for something
it seems you should remember,
but a Diamondback rattles you away
from this place you know was always his
and leaves you just a scattered hint
of something out of freeway time.

— Richard Lasater

THE CHIHUAHUAN

Two hours out of Deming
your horse went lame,
made an anachronism of your day
while August sands burn
this Chihuahuan Desert stark.
Cholla and centipedes try
to anchor life
and green you see in Creosote
brush is just another shade of dry.

Nights, even desert oven temperatures
fall with the sun
and when the moon reflects
the sand fills with tracks.
Coyote yelps and owls
haunt the air.

Feelings you can’t fit
tell you Pegasus landed here
when this edge was ocean.
He left his tracks forever in the wind
and the ocean left crinoids
for Cub Scouts
and Paleontologists.

Now bulldozers
ravage, scar and claw
marks cling for decades
and the roasted sky pulls back
to wait for storms and winter.

Two hours out of Deming.

— Richard Lasater

DISTANT VALLEY

The browning wind blows,
rough, dried and cracking,
through the olive branch
nailed across my door.

One greying dove
with a twisted grip
clings to perch
and prune where feathers
are no more.

And wind-swept rumors
have carved a solid base,
knot an image flashed
from my guts
of faceless facing
armies, swords arcing
across some distant desert valley
eroding through my home.

— Richard Lasater

LIKE MY SON AWAY FROM HOME

I backpack this canyon
John Park drew, once
I wrote it in a story
but, the red of the cliff
is never red enough
and the Blue River
has no force.

I talk of poems
that leaf out with sounds
like Sycamores in Spring,
explore my second
son's exploring
while my first son sprawls
across my mind
scanning the sky
for those Canadians up there
lost between seasons
like my son
away from home
in a place
I know well
in this poem.

Your cries
ripple my back as grass
shapes me where I lie.
Searching the faint geese sounds
I squint into pale Northern sky
empty but for you,
distant, undulating
ribbon of silver wings.
You veer from where you go,
veer back and then go on.
You rush to horizons
forever changing
never reached.
You are somewhere
between
lost and free,
driven by some reason
not understood.
Your call across the sky
an echo, lonesome
for where you've been
and where you want to be.

for Shaun

— Richard Lasater

A Different Good-bye

Richard Lasater

July in Texas is a bitch, but that Sunday morning a soft breeze, smelling damp and green, blew a little relief through our North Houston suburb. The pecan tree I'd transplanted three years ago when we moved in appeared to have taken root and heart and was looking like a survivor.

It was already too hot to get interested in mowing the carpet-grassed lawn I'd struggled to keep in the expected uniform of this neighborhood, but I persisted even though my thoughts drifted: to a cold Coors beer, to a long shower, to my last good trip to Colorado and the Poudre River Canyon. But persisting with the yard work was necessary; it was my excuse for not attending church with Becky and the kids.

Glancing at the home of my down-the-street neighbor, George Reynolds, I hoped he wouldn't wander out with a beer for me, and conversation. The other night he'd drunk a few too many and talked freely, said he and Judy had fought most of their thirteen-year marriage. Hanging his head, thin shoulders hunched, he quietly claimed he could not get out of it, debts and kids and such being the reasons. George said she nagged at him on every issue and got angry over everything he did or did not do: from the way he smoked too much, the job change he didn't make, the clothes he didn't like, the alley cat he fed, to not keeping the yard or not fixing it the way she thought he should want to.

He described well his anxiety, said every day it was part of him like an elbow with rheumatism, the awareness of it always at the edge of consciousness and sometimes a grinding pain. It gnawed at him; his stomach felt like a rat was in it gnawing, always gnawing. Once in a while when the gnawing stopped it felt so peaceful it was scarey, like he'd lost part of himself.

I didn't want to talk to George for a while; I felt shifty-eyed around him. I'd suggested that he and Judy should talk or go get help or maybe face facts. I'd admitted that Becky and I didn't always agree. I hadn't mentioned the rat in my own guts or that maybe Becky and Judy had a point to their views.

The yells of the Carson kids across the street pulled me back to Sunday morning yard work and away from hard confessions and dark thoughts. They, the Carson kids, fought happily as they rode their bikes and trikes all over the sidewalk and driveways. Whining from down the block, an electric lawn mower sang of another husband who mowed to escape church.

A Mockingbird in the pine tree by our den window switched songs about every three seconds, just like my thoughts. How long had I been a Mockingbird fan—thirty-seven years? And thoughts painted pictures of gravel roads, Dad's old '49 Mercury, boys playing through endless summers, and gut knotting problems such as how to ask Dot Montgomery if she wanted to go get a Coke. The Mockingbird switched songs again and I remembered young ones, fallen from nests, I'd tried to raise.

It flew, the Mockingbird, when the door slammed. I turned, saw Judy Reynolds cut across her yard at a dead run, head up the middle of the street. Her high heel shoes clacked the cement, flopped at funny angles—I thought she'd run clear out of them—and her tight green skirt rode up past her beige slip. Her face looked like a newspaper photoshoot of the finish of a long race, the shot of the loser that almost won.

I thought I saw my name on her lips just before George stepped out from his front door in that unhurried long striding way of his. The only thing different about George was the long-barreled Winchester twelve gauge bird gun in his hand.

It seemed like dream in slow motion, Judy reaching out, the odd angle of her left shoe's heel, George's shotgun coming to his shoulder, the second blast—blasting through the echo of the first, thundering as if lightening had split the shimmers of heat rising from our very street, and Judy still reaching out.

She seemed to leap, forming a dive that belly flopped on the oil and rubber-stained street, skidded what seemed like twenty feet, started up in a crawl, and then just folded. I'm glad I couldn't see her face.

In what seemed like the hazy distance, I saw George turn in his unhurried way and walk back into his house.

The only movement when I got to her was the blood trickling from her nose and ears and the meaty cavern quivering in her back. I don't remember getting the quilt from our bed or covering her. The constant echoing of the blasts wouldn't let me think.

When I talked to George in jail he said he didn't want visitors, said the gnawing was gone.

I told Becky I'd try to help her keep the house when I moved out about three months after Judy's funeral. She didn't seem to hear me, or maybe believe me, or care. That's okay, I understand. It hasn't been easy for me either. I spend a lot of time listening to Mockingbirds switch songs and hearing shotgun blasts echo in my head.

RICHARD LEE LASATER grew up in the south Texas sulfur fields, a landscape reflected in the poetry he began writing at 35. He and Rose met when they were both parole officers. They have been married 30 years and share a love of language and writing.

ROSEANNE LASATER has always been a wordsmith, starting as a reporter and feature writer in the press, then as a speech writer, grant writer . . . the business card said, "Putting words to work for you!" Now retired from state service Roseanne is working on a novel.

After the Gleaning

We dropped anchor in a deserted bay,
paddled the dinghy to a little cove;
you took off my clothes;
ocean rocked us to sleep.
It seemed so simple, how could I know
You would turn away?

All the empty jars that line these
rough unpainted shelves were once full.
They made a show,
contentment in a row of yellow peaches,
applesauce brown as cinnamon stick,
tomato juice bright and plum butter
dark amber of molasses.
Spicy salsa everybody raved about
is all gone . . . there was never enough.

Now spiders and dust weave
their pervasive veil
over all these empty jars.
Cellar air is damp,
musty scent clean enough,
but glass rims don't gleam.
Nothing about them invites touch.

I remember them full.
I remember gathering fruit,
peach bloom itchy on my skin.
I remember how you always loved
to eat my home-canned fruit
and one you wouldn't let me pick

Your suitcase stuck up like a rock
in the hall, by the door.
I held myself tight, watched you leave;
heard the rocking chair squeak,
said nothing, but when you were gone,
I sat a long time, talking to myself.

This house has a root cellar.
Heavy wood door on a rusty metal ring,
like the loop in an oxen's nose.
Stone stairway down beneath the porch
below the kitchen, cellar walls,
carved from solid stone,
rough and lumpy
like the inside of a cave.
This house is built on rock.
It is not my house, but it has a plum tree.
When the plums ripen, I will pick them.

It's quiet below ground. Spiders own this part,
an old country house in an old country town,
with windows that stick and walls that run
at odd angles to each other
. . . an easy house to live in.
A piece of broken cardboard box
makes a dry mat on the dirt floor where,
when all the jars are empty
it's good to have a quiet place to sit.

Shy women in white robes
lined up along the wall, outside
the door where the machine was.
I remember how nobody was there,
they all left without a word
when the machine was turned on.
Later we drank juice and averted our eyes.

— Roseanne Lasater

Light

Out of nothing, a seed
not a tree, not an apple
Just potential

Out of nothing, a drop
not an ocean, or a puddle
Just possibility

Out of nothing, a note
not a concerto, not a chord
not a song

Out of nothing, an egg
not a bird, not a chick
Just the hope

Out of nothing, an idea
not a book, not a sentence
Just a thought, a flicker

Out of nothing, a light
piercing the darkness
confounding obscurity

Frances Archer

Exordium: a beginning or introduction especially to a discourse or composition.

Synonyms: foreword, intro, introduction, preamble, preface, prelude, prologue. **Etymology:** Latin, from *exordiri* to begin, from *ex-* + *ordiri* to begin.

The following pages contain the introductory chapter or chapters from selected contributing authors of this anthology.

M. Kari Barr introduces an alternate world within our own. A world peopled with Fairies, Elves and Dragons, in modern times. *Once Again: Tales of Destiny* is truly an exordium into a whole new realm. The series is projected to include six volumes, rich enough to become thoroughly immersed in a different reality.

May Cotton offers a prelude to a fully engaging look into her life from the 1950's and onward. Her memoir focuses on interactions within her family, notably her experiences growing up with a sister who was born with developmental disabilities.

Wayne Kyle Spitzer shares the beginning chapters of his story detailing life in small town U.S.A. namely Spokane, Washington. This coming of age story has all the feels and nostalgia one needs to declare it a true masterpiece.

Once Again

Tales of Destiny

Book One

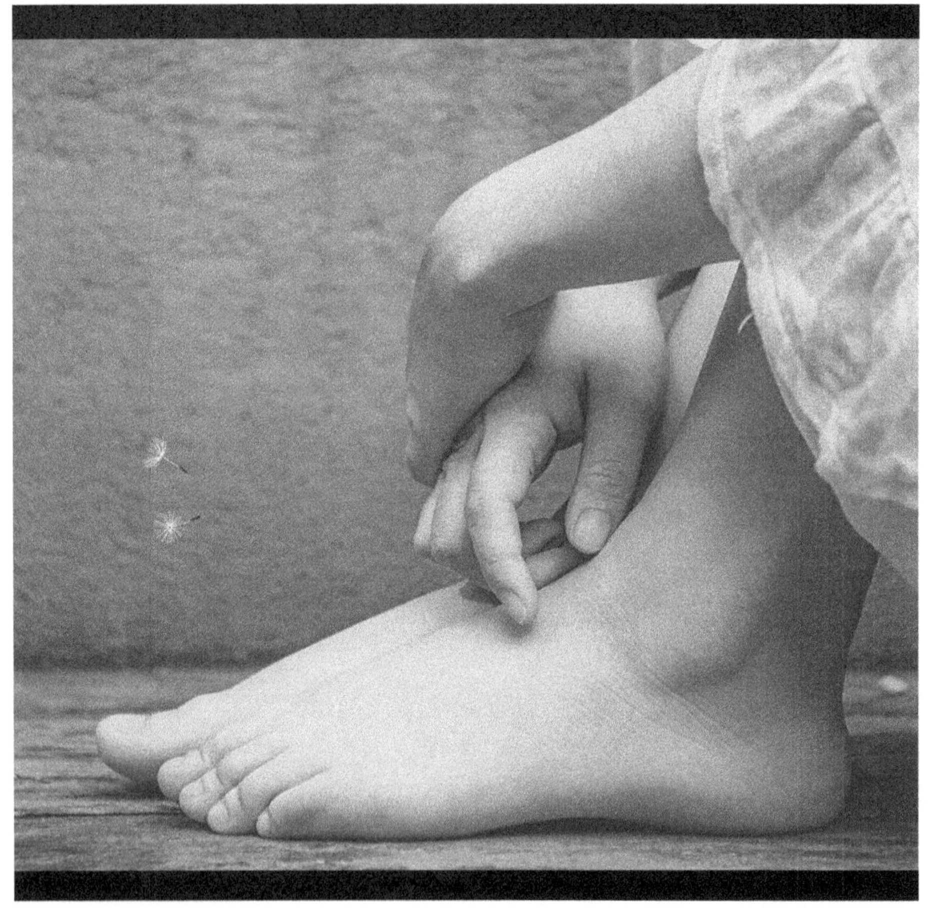

M. Kari Barr

Mara as told in her own words

The city bus arrived. After boarding, I turned toward the window to gaze at the scene one last time. The guy I dubbed 'Mr. Sunshine' glanced up and smiled—rakishly.

Back then I practiced the art of denial. I was unlike any of my classmates. In a way, I felt ostracized. All my young life weird experiences happened to me, things no one else noticed or saw. By eight or nine I had learned to keep my mouth shut; except, of course, for talking to myself. I came to accept that others did not see glitter floating through the air, or light emanating off of people. Never mind ogres and trolls. Over the years I barely even registered seeing these things anymore.

For my eyes alone, Mr. Sunshine exuded first a golden aura followed by a purple afterglow that I found particularly enchanting. *Admit it, Sweetie, the reason photography captured you as a little girl was to prove to Mom that fairies are real,* I had thought. With fervent effort, my younger self had tried every trick I could contrive, yet I never came upon a camera or f-stop setting that could capture the authentic auras witnessed daily.

Triggered by the golden glow given off by Mr. Sunshine, a swift succession of images flashed through my mind that day—

In the garden at age three: Daddy pointing at a pair of tiny shoes beneath the ferns in the backyard. The shoes swiveled back and walked deeper into the shadowed green. Daddy chuckled and held me tight before kissing my brow and setting me down.

I re-experienced being in first grade during the third week of school: Leaving the lunchroom, a raucous clatter sounded when a lid fell off a trash can. Turning around, a scream escaped my lips as an ogre dressed in the janitor's clothes cussed and picked up the lid. The humiliation and taunting of my classmates made me sick for a week.

At Daddy's memorial service: The entire world glowed with fairy lights, but especially at the cemetery. Most of the guests emitted light, some had wings. And the air swirled with glitter and scents so sweet I would have cried because it enchanted me so. But I was already crying. Little people—I had been told by my father that they were brownies, fairies, and wind sprites—hid in the lilacs nearby. Little people that my mother said did not exist.

"They don't exist," I quoted by rote.

With a slight shake of my head to clear my mind, I dispelled the images in order to deal with the reality of work

Aerrvin as told by Bronwyn

It wasn't as if he'd meant to sound petulant. Aerrvin couldn't have asked for a more faithful servant as found in Bronwyn MacIntash. Making a scene on the beach showed a petulance not often revealed. Most days he was his own Purple self. He loved the qualities of being a Purple Fairy; it allowed him to be more playful and carefree. In his opinion, it was better than being Yellow, like his sister.

Ah, Harmony, he thought as he lounged upon the shore, *she's the one at fault. Without her demands, I would not have yelled at Bronwyn at all.*

***

"I am not selfish! I simply want to do as I please, is that so hard to understand?"

"No, Aerrvin, I understand you. I do. It is just—hmm, you are turning one hundred and ninety years old next month, and you have yet to find a bride. Your parents are beginning to despair, and for them, that is saying something! You know how patient they are," the broad Brownie sighed but kept a steady eye on his charge.

"I know, I know! If tha' sister o' mine had waited a pint-size longer t'marry, they would not be ever fretful!" In his frustration, his Irish accent grew thick. "Aye, she be t'cause of all me woes!"

Splashing his foot in the tide pool, Aerrvin appreciated the musical sound as he witnessed the sun catching the liquid diamonds before they rejoined the small impression in the sand. Becalmed, he continued, "Just because tradition says the oldest must have a child first, doesn't mean it must be so. Does it?"

"Well, sir if I may say so, such a thing has never been done. Do you wish to break tradition, just to see what happens?"

Bronwyn had a point, so Aerrvin agreed to think upon it. The Brownie removed himself a respectful distance away. Each appeared in his natural state, being roughly six inches in height. Bronwyn climbed onto a piece of driftwood and settled down to whittle some delicate whimsy.

Situated between the two starfish in the tide pool, Aerrvin wriggled to find the most comfortable position. He visualized how he looked as his golden hair swirled in the ripples. His vanity showed on his face at the thought. Though truth be told, Bronwyn sat busily carving that very scene from the driftwood upon which he perched. The rendering would attest to the beauty of the fair prince as his hair danced in unison with the sea urchins and anemones.

The tide inched its way up each half hour, so Aerrvin dared himself to come to a decision before the pool became a part of the ocean herself. Stroking the nubby surface of the purple starfish on his right soothed his anxiety over having yelled at Bronwyn. Not only was he Aerrvin's personal servant, but the Brownie was also his royal historian and advisor. Brownies are brilliant at most any task they are given and are excellent writers. Aerrvin allowed it was quite disrespectful to lash out against him. *Here! Here!*

The truth of the matter was that Aerrvin was also partially White in his genetic make-up, causing him to cycle out of his happy-go-lucky moods from time to time. Being in a White Fairy mood meant that Aerrvin felt a need to withdraw from social contact. Sometimes he hid away for days, other times months. During these cycles, all beings learned that he was best left alone. Even so, being in a White frame of mind meant he could ponder more clearly, and make wiser decisions. It was deemed a good trait for a future King to have.

Entering The Land of Dreams within the Void, Aerrvin chose to visit long-past memories—*events, dear reader, which he chooses to keep to himself at present. Suffice it to say he pondered upon each fair maiden he had known up to this point.*

As the tide neared its highest mark, the delightful Wind Sprite, Mirri Sihee—Aerrvin's constant and invisible-to-most companion—advised, "My Lord, I do agree, tis time for you to put aside your childhood. If I could wed thee, I surely would, as well you know. But go, make a legend of your search, one worthy of the bards in olden times."

Delight warmed his soul causing a small fit of joy to bubble out. "Ha! Mirri you are the light that cheers my soul. How could I find anyone who could compare?"

Aerrvin hugged his precious companion and nodded; his chin tapped softly against her iridescently sheer shoulder. Then lying back down upon the starfish whereon they lay he continued, "But yes, you are correct: 'Tis time and time enough to be sure."

Mirri Sihee ran her feather soft fingers through his golden locks; breathing sweet songs of peace into his soul.

With a mental sigh, Aerrvin rose up out of the tide pool. The young Fairy Prince squared his shoulders as he prepared to upsize to full Human proportions and proclaim his willingness to comply.

In Honor of Our Queen
And for the Enlightenment
of Mankind

Bronwyn of Clan MacIntash

1

Picture Perfect

And if our dreams should go awry, what then my sweet, what then?
~ Morvayne ap Stewart

Thursday, May 7, 2009

For Mara, only one thing filled her life with meaning: her art. Photography consumed her imagination. With her camera, she felt she could make a difference in the world.

But it wasn't true. Nothing she did could bring him back. None of her pictures captured the proof she sought. The college student had nothing else to cling to, so she allowed her passion for photography to consume her.

Mara stood at the crossroads of life that day—unaware of the many eyes trained upon her. The destiny of that single young woman balanced upon a pin, a destiny that would affect the lives of everyone. Those watching noticed that Seattle's morning hum barely filtered into her consciousness as she walked to the corner to catch the bus. Stop and go traffic, belching exhaust from passing buses, and nearly getting run over by an angry bicyclist did nothing to sway her intense focus.

Swiping a dark curl out of her eyes, Mara spoke to herself, "Hmm, the assignment is to photograph unique images that represent nature in the city. Nature in the city—nature, natural, hmm." Unable to come to a decision for her college final, she emitted an explosive sigh of exasperation.

Mara's face brightened as she neared her bus stop in front of an old, vacant laundromat, bustling with new life. Workers were taking boxes into the building from a truck. She settled lightly on a nearby bench, seemingly enchanted by the blond in particular. Since her camera was already in her hand, Mara snapped a few shots to add to her photo journal. An annoying translucent Wind Sprite kept blocking Mara's view. Exasperated, she grabbed it around the waist and flung it aside, ignoring its protests as easily as she had ignored the bicyclist. Adjusting the zoom, Mara soon captured the object of her interest.

In the afternoon sun, an aura of gold emanated away from him for a moment. Her next sigh was vastly different from her previous one.

That was when her bus arrived. Most of her watchers followed Mara to work and later back home, once again. Yet, one alone remained, intent on knowing more about this golden boy.

May 8, 2009

"Friday," Mara said, smoothing her curls in front of the mirror. "Today, I turn in my idea for photography. And I have a calculus test. I hate math!"

Hastily, she applied a pale pink blush and a light skiff of brown eyeshadow to accentuate her lavender blue eyes. "No time for mascara, I might miss the bus," she murmured as she rushed out of her room.

Mara's housemate caught Mara mumbling, she quipped, "Talking to yourself again?" Jill rented the bedroom suite across the hall. They shared Mara's house, inherited from her beloved great aunt.

"Not any more than usual," Mara replied as the two went downstairs for breakfast. "What are we doing tonight?"

"A block party to welcome our new neighbors!" Jill shimmied down the stairs and into the kitchen.

"I am woefully ignorant of any new neighbors, but it sounds fun," Mara responded, grabbing an orange and a granola bar.

Mara's lack of enthusiasm and odd vocabulary caused Jill to roll her eyes at her younger housemate.

Offering Jill a shrug and a smile, Mara went out the door. She walked the half block to the bus stop, but she was earlier than needed, so she walked further down the street to the old laundromat on the next corner.

"Just to check on their progress," she mused. A small, twisty smile pulled at her mouth. She was lying to herself but wasn't ready to admit it. Mr. Sunshine's smile from the day before still played with vibrant color in her mind.

2

A Gentle Breeze

Then breathe my sisters, through the trees, let us sing the songs of life.
~ Mirri Sihee

Thursday, May 7, 2009

Aerrvin felt her energy as soon as she arrived outside the store. He and his cousin were carrying boxes inside. *Oh, now this girl likes me. A lot. She looks pretty sweet herself.* The upsized Fairy couldn't help wanting to catch her attention with magic. *Flipping Somersaults, what can I do?* He had his personal scent which some found attractive, of course, but he didn't have time to waft it towards her. Before he could do anything, she turned and boarded the bus.

He knew a Human could not see Fairy Light, but his vanity caused him to flash his Purple and Golden Brilliance to the world when he felt her emotions brushing against his soul.

Aside from those two mystical means for garnering attention, Aerrvin considered that the only other course of action was just that—action. Chancing boldness, he found her gaze as the bus pulled away. Her thoughts were intense, and Aerrvin couldn't help but offer his most practiced smirk.

After the bus pulled away, Aerrvin asked Gareth, "Did you see her? She's *The One*."

Gareth, wearing his black hair in a quasi-bun, stopped to stare at his golden-haired cousin. The two looked identical, apart from hair color, and strangely enough, the pair had been born on the same day. Much like twins, they were close to inseparable. And again, like many twins, their personalities were quite different.

With eyebrows raised, and his Irish accent not yet moderated to American, Gareth asked, "Why the rush? We have yet to spend two nights in the city!"

"Then I must assume that you did not see her," Aerrvin replied. "Her stunning looks rival Athena's. But more than that, the Aeries love her. Right, I know the Aeries do not reveal themselves to you. But trust me, the Wind Sprites danced around her like a sweet flower in the meadow, even pulling at her hair. Of a truth, she cast one aside!"

Busily unpacking boxes, their companion, Jaera, rolled her eyes. Unable to hold her tongue, she said, "Crikey, Aerrvin, you must have imagined it. We all know a Human can no more control a Wind Sprite than they can sprout wings and fly. You canna' marry the first Human ta strike your fancy. Marriage is serious business."

With a shake of her head, Jaera strode away to shelve the newly unpacked items.

Very well, I will bide my time and allow things to play out as they will, Aerrvin thought.

Aerrvin beckoned Mirri Sihee with a wriggling come hither motion of his hand. Few are blessed to see Aeries, but the young Fairy Prince happened to be one such blesséd soul. Once the Wind Sprite was close enough for him to whisper to, he said, "Ask those Sprites why they like that girl so much."

Then raising his voice as Mirri flew away he called, "And learn her name—and where she lives!"

May 8, 2009

"Hey, Aerrvin, that girl you like is outside," Gareth called. "Why do you think she is *The One*?" He raised his hands gracefully for dramatic effect. Aerrvin joined Gareth at the window.

"Magic," Aerrvin replied in his rich Irish accent.

"Oh, no 'tis not fair, nor allowed," Gareth said. "Compulsion is strictly forbidden. Is that not right, Jaera?"

"Sure as my hair is red, but I doubt he used Compulsion. Did you?" With decided poise, Jaera balanced on the topmost step of a ladder, hanging chimes on hooks attached to the ceiling. She faced Aerrvin with her impish lips pursed—awaiting his reply.

"No, of course not. I am high-born and well-schooled. I used an old spell learned from my great-grandfather before he Faded, great is his memory; it makes me *aware* of someone when they think about me. I can even feel the emotions they emit. Quite useful among, say—friends and enemies." Aerrvin paused to glower at Jaera. He held no real grudge against her, but as younglings, Jaera often tried to get Aerrvin in trouble with their teachers.

"It usually only works on those in whom I have an interest, be they friend or foe, and they must be within twenty spans or so."

"Limited, but useful," Gareth said. "Will you teach me?"

"Later. Mirri says her name is Mara, and right now I sense this sweet Mara thinking pleasant thoughts about me."

The golden-haired Fairy smiled. Mara's thoughts were a touch stronger than pleasant, and Aerrvin liked the passion and hunger she projected. He picked up a wind chime and went outside to hang it on the new post installed for that very purpose. Above the post, a bronze plaque advertised the name and nature of the store.

In truth, Aerrvin could not say why he found her attention any more compelling than the girls he met at the club the night before, or the girl staring at him from the curb. The sandy-haired girl on the curb willed him to look at her. Yet she didn't garner his attention. *She wants me, and is miffed that I won't look at her,* he thought. *This dark-haired beauty has emotions bouncing all over the place.* A kind of sorrow echoed deeply, beyond his ken. *She's a puzzle I feel compelled to solve.* Suddenly Aerrvin felt a secondary stab of malice and despair aimed at him, but it was so swift and brief he could not pinpoint who projected it.

****

"*The Craftsman's Majick*. Perfect! Precisely what we need!" Mara exclaimed, raising the uninterested heads of her traveling companions for a moment. Mara rarely spoke directly to her fellow commuters, so it didn't surprise her watchers that those nearby merely glanced or nodded at her and went back to their own pursuits.

In silence for a change, she wondered, *does my angelic Mr. Sunshine work here or is he just a delivery guy?* Then to her surprise and delight, he walked out and looked sidelong at her with a secretive smile gracing his face. He proceeded to hang a wooden wind chime on a hook. A sudden puff of air blew his golden locks up off his collar and danced through the pipes, causing the chimes to sound: sweet and mellow.

"Beautiful," Mara marveled as the bus arrived.

A fresh scented sea breeze wafted towards her. With reluctance, Mara boarded and took her customary seat halfway back. Closing her eyes, she almost saw an afterimage of a tiny form dancing among the chimes. In her mind's eye, she saw the breeze lifting the angelic store clerk's hair up off his collar. Firmly shaking her head to dispel the fantastical imagery, she exhaled a musical swoon.

"Now, why didn't I take a picture?!" Mara whispered on the crowded bus. "Oh, I've got it! My final project will be about the effects of wind in the city. I'm glad I only have two classes today. I can't wait to begin!"

Her seatmate nodded absently. She'd sat with Mara before.

****

Mara captured simple images: the flag extended by the breeze, students brushing hair out of their eyes, a seagull hovering in place on a warm current of air. She went to the docks to get the wind on the water. The blustery afternoon offered spectacular shots of sails puffed out and quintessential white caps. In a parking lot, she managed to spy a particularly artful arrangement of windswept trash flung up against a chain link fence.

"Edgy—definitely edgy," she mused in satisfaction. In time, her wandering brought her back to her side of town where she once again stood in front of *The Craftsman's Majick*.

"Are you going in or not?" Mara questioned herself. "Yes, of course, I am," she answered.

Inside, the musty laundromat appeared to have undergone a magical transformation. Bright swaths of jewel-toned silk billowing down the walls offered a cheery effect. Mara felt like she had won a prize as she walked from row to row. With delight, she found photography supplies. Not many craft stores carried them, so with abandon, the photography student selected several things needed to restock her darkroom and even some she did not. Precariously balancing her items, she got in line to make her purchase. Looking ahead for Mr. Sunshine, her countenance fell.

"So he doesn't work the counter, after all," she whispered.

As she waited, she watched a tiny red-haired teen straightening the shelves. At the register, an efficient woman with sandy brown hair and warm eyes turned her attention towards Mara.

"My! What an armful," remarked the cashier. Her nametag read, "Button."

Unable to stop herself, Mara blurted, "Your name is Button?"

"Why yes it is, and a finer name I've never had."

Someone behind Mara sniggered. Blushing, Mara pulled out her debit card and completed her transaction in silence. On her way out the door she muttered, "Mm, that didn't go so well."

"What didn't go so well?" asked a decidedly smooth voice.

Feeling the humiliation crawl up her neck, Mara turned back. There he stood next to the wooden wind chimes; the wind once again fluttered Mr. Sunshine's hair as the soft melody sounded: vibrant and clear.

With a catch of her breath, she stammered, "Oh, ah—I—I think I offended your boss."

"*My* boss?" he asked with a single raised brow.

"Yes. I've never heard of anyone named Button before," Mara replied, gaining composure.

"Never you mind. Button is an old family. . ." he twisted his lips in thought before continuing with, "friend. And a sweeter lady you will never meet."

With a nod at her full arms, Aerrvin offered, "Would you like help with your packages? I do believe I am going your way."

"You are? Sure, I guess I did go overboard. I got so excited when I saw all the supplies I needed. I couldn't help myself." Mara handed over the larger of the two bags, shifted her backpack to a more comfortable position, and headed up the block. As they crossed the street in silence, Mara felt his gaze on her from time to time.

"I am somewhat afraid to tell you my name—since you go about offending people with unusual appellations . . ." he began.

Mara interjected, "Oh, no! Whatever name, my name is Mara, Mara Jamis."

". . . and I am Aerrvin ap Rosewin," he finished with a half turn, and extinguishing the impulse to bow, he flourished his free hand—without her notice. Watching to see her reaction he waited, both eyebrows raised, and a near-smile tickling his lips.

"Ah, yes, I've never heard that one before, but it suits you. You've got a slight accent. Where are you from?"

"My friends and I moved here from Ireland some time back. We have a place on the peninsula, but I wanted to try my hand as a businessman; so I opened the craft store. I am excited to see how it goes."

In shame, she covered her face with one hand; Mara did not think she could be more embarrassed. *The store belongs to him!*

"Sooo, Button works *for* you?" Mara cringed, not hearing his reply.

After turning up the sidewalk to her house, instead of fumbling for her key Mara rang the bell for Jill to open the door. Projecting calm, she turned to face Aerrvin, still sporting that slight smile on his charming face. His eyes pierced her soul. He nodded with the fluid grace of a martial artist bowing to his master and then handed Mara her bag. Her heart thundered.

As he turned away, he called back, "I'll see you tonight."

Jill opened the door and gushed, "Oh, sweet! You met the new guy down the street. Isn't he ca—ute?"

Still mortified, Mara moaned, "He's coming to the party?"

****

Jill made a big production out of her parties. Her friends across the street were often invited to set up their mondo bulky speakers on the patio.

The young neighborhood never complained about noise.

As a sous chef with intentions of opening her own catering business, Jill's food never failed to delight and amaze. The only thing she allowed Mara to help with was decorating.

"I found inspiration at the craft store, Jill, I hope you don't mind. I'm hanging these gauzy curtains all around the gazebo. I want to get a few creative shots of the wind catching the curtains."

"No problem, kid. Do you want Dougie to bring his colored lights to shine on them?" Jill asked, rubbing dough from her fingers into the sink.

"Sure, that would be awesome."

At 6:00 p.m. and satisfied with her work, Mara made her way into the kitchen. The gazebo already had white Christmas lights spiraling up the columns and around the perimeter of the scrollwork below the roof. Mara's Great Aunt Lily had kept a stunning flower garden, and often hosted tea parties with her niece and grandnieces. As a result, Mara held fond memories of the gazebo and ensured that she kept the yard up to Aunt Lily's standards.

The yard was small, but lovely considering they were right in the middle of the ever-growing Seattle-Tacoma-Bellevue megalopolis. Spring in Seattle is not the best time for outdoor parties with a significant amount of success. Rain might fall at any given moment, but it had been sunny, and the temperature remained pleasant at seventy-one degrees.

The covered patio and the two oversized French doors connected the outdoors with the dining hall. The dining hall stood empty because Mara had sold the antique dining set to pay for that year's tuition. Overall the place was large enough to host thirty or so of their closest neighbors and friends, which Jill would do every week had Mara not put her foot down: two parties a month maximum.

"Okay, I'd better get cleaned up," Mara said. "How about you, Jill, are you done making all your goodies?"

"Almost, one last batch of mini quiches and then I'm done. Don't use up all the hot water!" Jill called out as Mara ran past to avoid the sponge in Jill's upraised hand.

Each reveled in using up as much hot water as they could stand; it was the one real contention between them, but even then they rarely ever ran out.

****

"And what is the dress standard for one of these "block" parties?" Aerrvin asked. The look of skepticism was not lost on Bronwyn as the two of them surveyed the contents of the prince's closet.

"Begging your pardon, Your Highness, it is not as though you are attending Princess Victoria's birthday party," Bronwyn replied. His nose, aimed at the ceiling, twitched. "It has been sixty years since our last excursion among Humans, and I am sorry to say, party clothes have gone downhill. You will wear no formal clothing tonight; simple jeans and a silk shirt for appearance's sake. This will have to do." Bronwyn cut short his opinion with a sniff and retrieved an outfit from the closet.

"Ah well, these jeans are not as comfortable as silk, but they do tend to grow on a body." Aerrvin's voice became muffled as he pulled on a gray muscle shirt to wear beneath his midnight blue shirt.

"Thank me little 'uns for that. Each night they wash 'em and wear 'em to soften 'em up. Next time have me wife Button make your jeans, rather than buying or acquiring them elsewise; then they will be perfect from the start!"

Aerrvin nodded in near sober agreement at his most trusted adviser. Both knew he might obey, but more than likely he would not.

"Now then, we are all set. Jaera, you look lovely as usual. What kind of shirt is that, Gareth?" Aerrvin scrutinized his cousin.

"It's flannel! Everyone wears it." He grinned. Then opening it up he proclaimed, "I even got the perfect t-shirt to go with it." Sporting a smug grin, he revealed a swamp green T-shirt with the Space Needle on it.

Aerrvin's eyebrows rose, touching the fabric he said, "Yes, it looks like flannel, but it's so thin and not made of wool. Very well then. Are you sure you do not want to come along, Bronwyn?"

"Oh, no. 'Tis quite all right with me. I'll stay home with Button and me lassies and reminisce about the time I did go to Princess Victoria's birthday party; you were mere babes then. Besides, I need young Seamus here to go and learn the trade. As I age, I will have a need to pass on the quill."

Bronwyn's middle child, Seamus, had been born one month after the prince. The two had grown up together and quite enjoyed each other's company.

"Now then, if you would shrink him to his proper five inches, and make him transparent so as not to cause the Humans alarm, Your Highness."

Bronwyn nodded as his invisible, shimmering son climbed to sit upon Aerrvin's shoulder using a hank of his hair to keep from sliding off.

Humans cannot see the shimmer unless their eyes are touched with magic. Brownies are rarely seen, even without an invisibility spell, because they are so adept at camouflage. They live in almost every home ever built. Truth be told, they would offer so much help if only people knew of their existence. Their primary task is to keep pests at bay, rats and Goblins being their foremost enemies.

"Seamus, you might need to braid a shank to make a more secure hold for yerself."

"Aye, Father." His fingers seemed to fly as he wove an intricate braid with the hair from behind Aerrvin's left ear. He finished by tying it up with a strand of gold thread.

With the ever-present Wind Sprite blowing his golden hair, Aerrvin and his companions set out to attend their first block party.

3

Of Golden Sunsets

Trailing feather-soft butterfly kisses across the sky, she paints kaleidoscopic splendor in the heavens.
~ Aerrvin ap Rosewin

Friday, May 8, 2009

Mara's house sat in the center of the block seven houses down from the Victorian mansion Aerrvin rented. The Fairies' love of the gentle humid air of Seattle emanated from their very beings; they radiated joy. It was not raining, but clouds were forming to the west. Aerrvin knew the sunset would be fantastic. He despised missing a single one—dusk being his favorite time of day.

Cold temperatures do not affect magical beings much, but the warmth of the sun infuses bliss into the soul. The current temperature held steady at sixty-nine degrees with no wind, except around Aerrvin, who, thanks to Miree, always brought a bit of a breeze wherever he went.

"Jaera, I think your Fairy Dust is a little overbearing." With a slight wave of Aerrvin's hand, a breeze sent a smattering of sparkles free. "You don't need much to garner attention among college students," Aerrvin admonished as he assessed her attire.

Jaera was a five-foot, fire-haired, freckle-faced imp of a girl and could get away with wearing her regular attire: pale green leggings with a filmy, flowing short top in shades of lavender and pink accented by a green scarf around her neck. She insisted she kept her curls cut short to make them bouncy. However, most agreed it was to keep her hair from getting tangled in the brambles which she so loved to climb. The only change to her wardrobe was a pair of strappy high-heeled sandals.

Aerrvin nodded to her shoes. "How easy is it to wear those, anyway?"

"As easy as dancing." Jaera twirled to prove her statement before resuming her natural bouncy pace beside Gareth.

Approaching the front door, Aerrvin slowed to look at his timepiece. They hoped to be fashionably late, but not too late, considering they were the guests of honor.

"Ah, here we go," Aerrvin said.

"You sound nervous, my friend," Gareth said with a grin.

"Have you tried to woo a wife?" Aerrvin asked, with a pointed stare at Jaera's backside and then back to Gareth as she rang the doorbell.

"Touché," Gareth replied with a lopsided frown. He kept Jaera as an option, but like all Fairies, making up his mind was hard. Still, Jaera remained his first choice.

Jill answered the door. "Yay! You're here! I'm so glad you came. Let me introduce you . . ."

The Fairy Prince scanned the room. Aerrvin's delight with the style and décor suffused him with a gentle glow. It felt homey. Upon entering the house, one could use either of the two coat closets left and right, then the rooms opened up to either side. To the left was a study with a luxurious brown leather sofa and two matching chairs. Burgundy curtains and pillows complemented both the leather and the navy blue carpet. *Positively cozy,* thought Aerrvin. On the right and on into the main hall, which should have been a dining room, the beautiful cherry wood flooring shone as with great care.

"Brownies live here, most assuredly," he mused under his breath.

"Aye," answered Seamus in his ear.

The living room to the right soothed the senses with its soft coloring contrasting the study. Guests sat on and around the pale lavender couches; some sat on the rectangular angora rug between the wraparound sectional. With a twinge of jealous emotion, Aerrvin noted guests idly handling the tactile silk and velvet pillows. The aubergine pillows accented the sofas beautifully. The mantel stood out on the western wall as the main feature of the room, marred somewhat by the large screen TV mounted above.

In the northwest corner sat a curious chair of evident antiquity. The chair had a grand high back, suitable for royalty. The cushioned seat and back were a beautiful shade of pale yellow, tufted with lavender buttons. The desire to sit in something that delightful made Aerrvin itch! Wriggling his shoulders, he continued his quick perusal of the room.

Near the fanciful chair sat a long buffet table, placed under the front windows and piled high with tempting treats. Aerrvin ensured that Jill knew that neither he nor his friends ate red meat. In the last corner sat a pile of large red, blue and purple pillows perfect for lounging on.

Still no sight of Mara. Masking his disappointment, Aerrvin greeted his neighbors as Jill introduced him to those in the room; then she excused herself to greet more guests. With one regretful glance at the chair, Aerrvin took the proffered pillow from Gareth and joined him, along with Jaera, on the floor in front of the other guests.

"Stay seated, you just got here," said a blonde girl.

She grabbed a friend, and they sashayed to the table where they filled plates with finger foods. A short, stocky man offered to get beers for the group.

"No, thanks. Water or milk for me," Gareth replied. The tone and clarity of Gareth's voice could capture the attention of all who heard it—to say it was musical would be an understatement.

Sliding her eyes sideways toward her friend, another girl went into the kitchen to inform Jill. Meanwhile, Jaera retrieved two lemon-lime sodas for herself and Aerrvin. Soda does not affect Fairies the way alcohol affects Humans, but the carbon dioxide itself was quite addicting to Fair Ones of any kind and induced cheer nonetheless. Gareth thought it altered his voice, so he did his best to avoid carbonated drinks. On the other hand, Jaera could not seem to consume enough.

The blonde and her friend returned with three plates and sat down on the floor beside Gareth and Aerrvin. "Here you are, sorry—seems to be all fruit and bread tonight. Jill always makes amazing stuff, though," Blondie said, as she picked up a fruit kabob.

"No problem. Seems all my favorites are here," Aerrvin replied, glancing over to see Gareth brush hands with the girl bringing him ice water.

"Sorry, no milk," she said, biting her lip.

Attracting attention is never a problem for Fairies and Elves. Making friends is as easy as drinking water and dancing. The problem for Aerrvin was making a commitment at all. A pull to befriend Mara washed over him. *She might be someone I could enjoy spending nine hundred or so years with. But all the girls and half the guys in the room are thinking about me. Granted, not all are pleased; some are jealous, of course.* A smile tickled his lips for a moment. He loved how the Ware Spell let him feel the strength of a person's reaction to his presence.

Not that he needed the spell to know the effect. With focus, he could hear the blonde girl's heartbeat and quickened breath; her sense of longing tantalized him. *Maybe I should sample more freely first.*

Offering a wry smile, he asked, "What was your name? I failed to pay attention during the introductions."

With a toothy smile of her own, she replied, "Bonnie Grant. I live one house down from you, I think. You're staying in the Victorian on the corner, right?"

****

Jill found Mara in the backyard. "Mara, you're ridiculous! You can't hide out here all night. It's not like he's judging you for misunderstanding his status. Who would think a twenty-something guy owned the place?"

"Yeah, yeah it's just that—I don't know. He's so cute he makes me nervous."

"Fine, stay here and take your pictures. I'm going to send people out to dance; it'll give you a few people to shoot." Jill paused and then added, "Doesn't look like you're getting much wind, though."

Mara realized she was acting childish. "But I do need to get these pictures. Let's see…" Raising her voice, she called, "Hey, Dougie, can you pose for me?"

Dougie was not model material by any stretch, but his craggy face presented a wind-etched appearance. Mara assumed it was from all the sailing he did on the weekends. She posed him on the garden bench after he adjusted his sound system for the umpteenth time. The weathered fence and flowering vines in partial bloom made an excellent backdrop. Twenty minutes remained before sunset, making ideal light and shadows.

"That's perfect, Dougie. Try not to smile. Great!"

"My turn, my turn!" claimed two fellow students from college. Jill had tried more than once to get Mara to go out on the town with either one of them, but Mara always had an excuse.

"Okay, let me think," Mara answered. "Oh, and thanks, Dougie, you were perfect."

He inclined his shaggy head as he backed away before returning to the house. Mara smiled to see a glimmer of happiness in Dougie's perpetually glum appearance.

Facing the guys, she said, "I'm trying to show the effects of wind in the city. I can't take many pictures until the wind picks up."

"How about a fan?" Joe asked.

"I thought about that, but it would be cheating. The pictures will mean more to me if they are authentic."

More people spilled out of the house to dance and enjoy the evening before it got too cold. A gentle breeze picked up the curtains on the gazebo right as Mara noticed Bonnie dancing with Aerrvin.

An involuntary gasp escaped. Squinting, Mara's lip protruded as Aerrvin took both of Bonnie's hands in his and swung her about jitterbug style. She turned back to Joe and ordered, "Get a girl with long flowing hair; I need a fantastic shot before the wind dies!"

"Yes, ma'am!" Joe snapped back with a smile.

In the meantime, Mara took several shots of the curtains dancing with the music, while studiously ignoring the peripheral rainbow hues she always saw flitting around when the wind blew. The sun turned from yellow to gold, causing the entire gazebo to appear as if on fire, or made of lustrous gold.

Time ceased when Mara became engrossed in her art.

"Fantastic," she breathed.

"It is," said that familiar smooth voice. "What are you doing, by the way? I mean, why are you always taking photographs?" Aerrvin asked.

Still taking pictures, Mara replied, "I'm a photographer. My final is due soon, and I need to get these shots before the wind dies."

Joe returned with Bonnie, the only girl at the party with waist-length hair.

Smiling to herself, Mara directed them to the center of the gazebo and asked them to pretend they were slow dancing despite the hip-hop pouring from the speakers. Amazingly, the wind behaved perfectly, the curtains billowed, and Bonnie's pale blonde hair shone gold as the sun settled to orange. The gentle breeze lifted her hair higher than seemed possible; the shot was brilliant.

Mara could not contain her joy. "This is so awesomely cool!"

Hearing a chuckle, she remembered Aerrvin stood behind her. She turned to look at him and saw the most beautiful sunset ever; the clouds covered half the sky. Brilliant oranges, pinks, and purples melted into each other. Aerrvin displayed as a silhouette against the light. While he stood facing the sunset, Mara admired his shoulder-skimming hair as it flowed away from his face. Without pausing, she continued snapping pictures. When he turned to face her, she stopped.

"Oops! Sorry, couldn't help myself," Mara explained as her face warmed. Pushing herself, she asked, "Would you mind standing in the gazebo so I can get a few more pictures? I would like to go around to the other side so I can get you and the curtains in the sunset. Please?"

Looking down at her, he inclined his head with a gentle nod and replied, "Not a problem, as long as I can watch the sunset." In reality, he was trying to comprehend her, but he maintained a calm façade.

While Mara moved to the eastern side of the yard, Aerrvin walked to the center of the structure. The music became smooth and calming. Gareth and Jaera found no difficulty in joining their companion in his evening ritual, so they sat out of the way on the gazebo stairs. Aerrvin stayed in the center the entire time it took the sun to descend. With the wind billowing the curtains in and out, Mara was confident she had captured grade A photos.

****

"Aerrvin," Seamus said in his ear, "would ye mind if I slipped down and visited with the Brownies? I am sure I can learn quite a bit about yer bride to be."

"Sure, and I'll even make you visible again. That Brownie lass under the fern there is rather fetching. For a Brownie," he amended with a mischievous twitch. "And Miree, tell your friends to cease their games in the curtains when Mara joins me."

"Aye, Love. But are ye certain she'll be joinin'?

Aerrvin shrugged.

****

Secretly pleased to witness Aerrvin talking to himself, Mara said, "So I'm not the only one."

Dusk settled; a pale pink glow remained, fading to purple. With a delighted laugh, Jaera grabbed Gareth and began delicately dancing about the yard. Gareth was pretty lithe himself; the form appeared to be a type of Irish jig, yet nothing Mara had ever seen.

Within minutes, they had everyone laughing and trying to copy their steps. Dougie turned on the colored lights, but after the spectacular sunset, nothing else compared. Mara took a few shots to honor the effort of putting them up and then decided to quit for the night.

Inhaling deeply, Mara spoke to Aerrvin, "Thank you. You don't need to stand there all night."

"'Tis quite all right. I can stand for hours adoring Helios."

Settling on the built-in bench, Aerrvin motioned for her to join him. The wind died down, the curtains blurred the view, softening the lights. "So, tell me about yourself." Interrupting as she started to speak, he asked, "Do you always host parties and then avoid your guests?"

Flabbergasted, she didn't know whether to be embarrassed or angry. "Well I have never—" she began, but before she could complete her sentence, Aerrvin took her hand and apologized. Her breath skipped as he stroked her hand, softly running his thumb across the back in a kind of circular fashion.

"I am sorry. That came out rude. Really, just—tell me about yourself."

Using her hands expressively, she exclaimed, "You don't come up to people and say: Tell me about yourself. What am I supposed to say? I'm in my last year of school. I work at the Safe Harbor Retirement Center four days a week. I have a mom, a step-dad, a step-brother and two half-sisters!"

She looked questioningly at him and charged, "Tell me about yourself."

His eyes sparkled as he pulled on his braid, sliding its silky softness through his fingers. Aerrvin answered, "You are right, you already know I own a craft store and come from Ireland. Ah, here's something; I have a mom, a dad, and one annoying baby sister. Not much to say. Come on; the night is young. Will you dance with me?"

****

Leaving the gazebo a few songs later, Mara shivered in the evening chill. Jaera and the others were relatively calm again. Getting drunk was strictly forbidden; Mara had kicked out guests before, and some never got invited back, not that they cared.

"Oh, I forgot my camera. . . " she started and then stopped as Aerrvin held out the strap for her.

Once inside, she realized it was 9:30 already. Maybe it was a little more than a few songs later. Still, it was relatively early as far as parties go. In the living room, Jill started a game of Pictionary, and in the study, Dougie's group of friends stood around looking at videos online.

"Hey, that's my new computer, guys. Don't break it!" Mara called.

Sudden sharp hunger pangs hit Mara, having not eaten since tasting one of Jill's mini quiches right out of the oven at 5 o'clock—and she'd missed lunch altogether.

Jaera stood on the edge of the living room with a plate of fruit and pastries, "Hungry?"

"Why yes, I'm famished." Mara gratefully accepted the plate and went into the living room to watch the game. Most of the pillows were taken, so she went to her favorite chair and carefully balanced the plate on her knees. When she realized that it left Jaera and Aerrvin without a seat, she started to get up.

Gathering the free pillows, Aerrvin said, "That's perfectly okay. I enjoy sitting at the feet of pretty women."

He flashed a twisted smirk. Jaera groaned, pinned him to the ground, and tousled his hair. The display was rather intimate, causing more than one raised eyebrow. Mara inhaled deeply, letting her breath out slowly. Jaera appeared quite green for a moment.

"Um, I have not had a chance to talk with you. Are you Aerrvin's little sister?"

Before she could answer, Gareth gracefully plopped between Jaera and Aerrvin and stole one of Aerrvin's pillows. "Not even close," Gareth said.

This comment set off another wrestling match, ending with Jaera on top, pummeling Gareth's chest with her tiny fists while he laughed uproariously.

"Sorry. I give, I give!" Gareth exclaimed, earning his release. He sat up to straighten his dark hair; a gentle shake and it fell silkily into place around his shoulders.

Mara was not used to such roughhousing. Her evident consternation worried Aerrvin, so he reached over to Mara's plate and took a carrot. Handing it to Jaera, he said, "No more soda."

"Yes, Father," she replied and then with a glance at Mara she piped, "No, he's not my father either. We grew up together, and Gareth is his cousin; I am Gareth's best friend, so where he goes, I go."

Gareth tugged on one of Jaera's curls. "Well said."

Meanwhile, Seamus returned, having waited behind a flower pot until acknowledged and transformed back to transparency. Once again sitting on Aerrvin's shoulder, he quickly informed Aerrvin about the darkroom in the basement.

Breathing deeply to relieve the pressure in his chest, Aerrvin felt gratitude for the tip. Jaera's antics made him feel perturbed. But his real worry was whether he was doing the right thing. On the outside, he was as smooth as could be. But inside he was a roiling mass of conflicting emotions. *If I did fall in love with her and she could not believe in magic, it would be one more heartache to add to my small collection of failed relationships. Ah, the pain!* Despite how he hated that pain, he nursed those emotions when feeling down, essentially spiraling into a bottomless abyss of self-torture. Now was not the time for such dark thoughts. He pushed aside his petty worries and watched Mara finish eating a fruit kabob. *Her lips are as luscious as that strawberry,* he thought. *How sweet and tender they must be.*

Licking his lips before addressing Mara, Aerrvin said, "We will have you over one of these days so we can get to know each other better. But for now, show me your darkroom." It was stilted, nearly a royal command; even so, he managed to refrain from 'shall and should.'

"How did you know I had a darkroom?"

"I carried your supplies this afternoon, remember?" A half-smile twitched on his expressive lips.

"Oh, yeah. I have had such a busy day! I can't remember half of it. Sure you can have a tour," she replied, inviting all three.

Jaera and Gareth declined. "No thanks," Gareth said, "I want to have a look at your computer. I need to get one myself." He fit right in with the geeks, most of Dougie's friends were dressed in flannel too.

Jaera thought Pictionary looked fun, so she went and sat on the nearest empty lap, earning sour looks from the girls sitting nearby.

The drizzle turned into an absolute downpour; Dougie and Jake came in with the sound system as Mara and Aerrvin walked past. Dougie gave her a polite nod.

****

In the kitchen, Jill busied herself with tidying up. She flashed her pearly whites and gave Mara a thumbs up as Mara motioned Aerrvin down the basement stairs. Mara couldn't remember the last time she had felt so out of control. Her heart was speeding, and she kept blushing. *Probably at senior prom. Did I really think Gerry Fink was all that?*

"Not even half," Mara murmured.

"What was that?" Aerrvin asked.

"Oh, not even half of the basement is complete. I've been remodeling. The house was built in 1890 and has a remarkably large basement—considering its age."

Two exposed walls revealed part of the basement foundation made of river rock and mortar. The room could have been a game room, but Mara did not care for pool or ping-pong. Wires ran along the walls, where photos hung from clothespins. It was bright and clean, with two counters—used for folding clothes—and pantry shelves beneath where Jill kept extra foodstuffs.

Embarrassingly to Mara, there sat two baskets of unfinished laundry, one washed and one not. While Aerrvin studied the photos, she hastily emptied the washer and started the new load.

"Okay, so this over here is my studio and darkroom," she said as she waved to the remainder of the basement. To the left, stood the door to the darkroom. The room was 10'x10'. Even though Mara used digital, she preferred the old-fashioned way of crafting pictures.

While developer does not necessarily smell good or bad, Mara always breathed in deeply when first entering the room. She associated the odor with the magic of watching pictures emerge; it gave her a thrill every time.

Mara's excitement became infectious. She exuded her love of photography in an almost tangible way. Aerrvin enjoyed her sense of aesthetics and delight. Her pictures were remarkable. In the red glow, Aerrvin picked up one of himself and Gareth moving boxes into their store; they were each wearing khakis and t-shirts. Gareth was saying something to Aerrvin. The photo captured the prince's mischievous grin, which he practiced for fifty years to perfect.

"You take magnificent pictures," Aerrvin said, jauntily sporting that same wicked grin. "Can I have this copy?"

Caught off guard again, Mara gasped softly; Aerrvin always looked as though he were posing for a picture. *How could such a perfect being be interested in me?*

She gave her head a shake to dispel the thought and replied, "Ah, yeah, yes—sure. Please, take any of these that you want. I've got one of Jaera, which she might like too."

"Can you show me how you develop a picture?" Aerrvin turned his attention to the counter while brushing up against her with seeming casualness.

Mara forgot to be self-conscious as she efficiently taught him the process. She even laughed at his jokes instead of blushing. As they came out of the darkroom, Jill entered the laundry room with dirty tablecloths and dishtowels. "Hey you two, it's after 11:30. Not that late, but most people have left, and Jaera has fallen asleep."

Heading for the stairs, Aerrvin said, "Poor Jae, she has not slept this past fortnight. I guess it's catching up with her."

In the living room, Mara found Jaera was indeed asleep, curled up on Kevin's lap. He did not look like he was too upset about it, but when he saw them, Kevin said, "It's about time you got here. I think my arm's asleep!"

The phone rang. Wondering who would be calling so late, Mara answered. Bronwyn was on the line saying that he was in the car outside. Not that they needed a car; Bronwyn just liked to drive. Mara relayed the message.

Aerrvin bent over Jaera to wake her. Once a Fairy crashes, it takes a lot to get them lucid. "Jaera? Can you get up? Oh, never mind. Gareth you take her. I'll get the door."

Gareth relieved Kevin of his burden and held her in the crook of his arm like a wee babe. He gave Jill and then Mara a hug with the other, "Thanks for the welcome party. We had so much fun…" Turning to another neighbor, he said, "…loved the dancing."

Outside, a sleek gray car with a black top waited. The driver got out, opened the back passenger door for Gareth and Jaera, and then stood to wait for Aerrvin.

Aerrvin hugged Jill, thanking her for the party and praising her culinary skills. Then he hugged Mara and kissed her cheek. "Thank you for the delightful company."

His near purple eyes lingered on her face a moment, and she felt her cheeks grow warm. Dropping her own lavender hued gaze, she managed a muffled, "Bye," as her fingers flew to her mouth.

Then the final partygoers all said their goodbyes and left.

"Yes!" Jill screamed, "I finally did it. I knew I could find someone to interest you!"

She hugged Mara and danced her around the room.

Mara smiled in return and replied, "I guess you do know what you are doing, and it only took you three years!" With a sarcastic smirk, she hugged Jill back.

Jill went to the kitchen to ensure the oven was turned off. With a sigh, Mara straightened the pillows in both front rooms. The leftover food could wait; they would finish cleaning in the morning. Mara had a habit of ignoring how much food was left because the next day it never matched up with her memory.

"Best not to think about it."

At the top of the stairs, she called out, "Good night, Jill."

Mara yawned, closing the door to her room. She thought about her preference to be particularly neat, so as not to cause extra work for the Brownies.

"Not that I really believe in them," she said to herself as she reached for her toothbrush.

Ever since she met a Brownie, whom she named Sylvie, when Mara was three years old, she had learned to put things back in their place. And Mara always cleaned thoroughly every Saturday. She hadn't spoken with Sylvie since she was five, so of course, she didn't really think it had happened.

"Just fairytales," she told herself, pulling on a cotton nightgown. Flipping off the light, she climbed into bed.

Her window looked out on the backyard where the lights from the gazebo remained on; a soft glow shone on her windowsill. With a smile, she remembered dancing in the gentle breeze behind the curtains. Falling asleep with her eyes open, she saw a tiny figure climb into the window.

"Sylvie," she breathed as her eyes slid shut.

The Introduction and first three chapters of *Once Again:Tales of Destiny* by M. Kari Barr (ISBN 978-1732140103) ©2018, used by permission of the author. Direct inquiries to bsdottr@gmail.com.

SISTER, SISTER: A MEMOIR

BY

MAY COTTON

2015: Beginning

"I've been reading your memoir over your shoulder as you write it," Ellen says as she sits down beside me on the bench overlooking the ocean. It is cold up here, but neither of us thinks of going in. We are bundled up, me wearing the warm woolen hat of creamy lavender knitted by Noela. Ellen wears the dark blue polar fleece Nordic cap I inherited from her, one of the few precious pieces of her past I still treasure. Usually it hangs on the post of the chevelle mirror beside my bed—on cold winter nights I wear it to sleep, though it always ends up on the floor after I begin to overheat.

"At least," Ellen continues, "the parts you've written since I died. I couldn't read before I died, but now I can. I read as you write. I love it when you read aloud to your writing groups. I love hearing your voice, hearing you tell your side of the story, feeling your pain and your shame and your love. I wish we could have been sisters like that when I was alive."

I look wistfully over at my dead sister, so radiant in her afterlife. "It wasn't possible then," I tell her. "I was too broken inside, and you were too broken outside." She nods and gazes out to the sea.

"How's Mom?" I ask.

"Oh, she's still over the moon about her book. Jumping for joy. Happy as a clam. All those euphemisms she used when we were growing up. She loves showing it to the ancestors whenever a member of the living picks it up to read. You really haven't been fair to her in this memoir, you know. She really was some kind of saint for all the crap she put up with from you and Tom, especially when she was trying to make up for being guilty of bearing the faulty gene that made me retarded.

"There, I said it. Are you happy now? Yes, that is what I was called then, and no, developmentally disabled in not poetic in the least. But you know you're going to get all kinds of flack for using that big bad R-word in your book."

"I know," I respond. "I get all bent out of shape when others take poetic license, but that's exactly what I'm doing. I know not everyone will understand. But to me it would be an anachronism to use current language to talk about what life was like in the 50s and 60s. We thought it was okay to use aberrant language then. We weren't so into avoiding hurting people's feelings by being so pathetically politically correct."

"But you know," Ellen tells me, a curious excitement in her voice, "you never called me a 're-tard', and you stood up for me when others used that awful word. I always appreciated that."

"I guess in some ways I wasn't such a bad sister."

"No, you weren't. You did your duty. You loved me before you learned to hate me, and that's worth a lot. You loved me enough to grow your heart bigger, and that early love prevented you from being as terrible as you might have been. And you only tried to kill me that one time."

"And I was unsuccessful, wasn't I? I'm just so glad I got over it in time to be able to love you again before you died. And I'd give anything to remember that early love, that first bloom of new sister."

"No you wouldn't. Never say you're willing to give anything. You never know what might be asked of you. You will remember what you need when the time is right, if not in this life, in the next. All is revealed in its own time. Neither you nor I have any control."

I look over at my sister and see she is wearing my multi-colored patchwork jacket, the one still languishing in the mending closet. All these things I know how to do, know I must do, visualize myself doing—but my hands have forgotten how, and my feet refuse to move me from the TV chair to the sewing chair where the tasks that await me seem never to begin.

Ellen interrupts my self-admonishing contemplations.

"You have no idea how I struggled to learn to say that word. It was such a big word, three syllables when it was hard for me say more than one. Your name was so hard. I was thrilled when you changed it to May. Do you remember I used to call you 'May Anne' because I couldn't say 'Mary'? It wasn't that I didn't know I was saying it wrong. I knew so much more than I could ever convey. I would have given anything—yes, I said it, even though I told you not to—I would have given anything to have gotten the surgery to release my tongue. It was so hard being tongue tied, not being able to move my tongue like a normal person. It was nearly impossible to keep my mouth closed. It was hard to eat; it was hard to speak.

"Some sounds, like the R in Mary were nearly impossible. And 'retarded' has two Rs! Then there was that third syllable. I struggled so hard with which syllable to emphasize, preventing myself from emphasizing the first to avoid that awful R-word. It took me years to learn to pronounce that bungled sentence you heard as 'I not retarded.' I knew what it meant many years before I could actually say it.

"I hope you understand I wasn't stupid. It's true I couldn't master reading and language, and I learned most everything at a slow pace, but I understood things, saw things, knew things you can't begin to understand. I chose to focus on the simple things, the fun stuff like bowling and football, so I could enjoy my life as much as possible. TV was easy, as you have discovered, because it told me stories. I just had to listen. It didn't matter much I couldn't read as long as the TV talked to me.

I reach over and pat my sister's hand. She is wearing Alice Walker's purple gloves from my 1987 trip to Big Mountain in Arizona, where I stood hand-in-hand with my then-favorite author as we protested the Federal government allowing strip-mining on sacred Navajo lands.

"But you can read now," I remind Ellen. "I see you've been reading my old journals. Otherwise how would you know about Alice Walker's gloves?"

"Oh, I hang around you more than you realize," Ellen says. "I can only read when you are reading or writing or what you leave open on the counters. But I hear you tell others your stories. You love your Alice Walker story, your connection to other writers who are famous now."

"At least Alice Walker and Maxine Hong Kingston were decent people," I blurt, "unlike that boob Bob Silverberg!"

Ellen chuckles at my indignation at this long-ago discovery that an author I idolized was nothing more than a crass man. I realize now that meeting male authors has always been a disappointment to me. The women are just so much more humble, more human maybe.

More human like Ellen is now, in her afterlife. I am glad she has come to sit with me on this bench overlooking the ocean. We will sit here together again, I think, and perhaps she will tell me more of her view of our sisterness, then and now.

X-Ray Rider 1

Mileposts on the Road to Childhood's End

Wayne Kyle Spitzer

Chronoscope | 1966—1972

HE LIVES in Spokane, Washington, a smudge of town just off the railway, a place rust-brown by day and elm-dark by night, filled with grain elevators and dim orange streetlamps; a place still without a freeway even in the late '60s. His immediate family consists of a mother and father, both in their forties, a brother, who is three years older, and himself. Because he is the youngest of seven boys—four from his mother's first marriage and a still-born between he and his brother—everyone calls him 'the Kid.'

They have a ritual which begins at the Phillips 66, in the late afternoon or twilight, where his mother buys him and his brother Cokes and candy cigarettes—Cokes in tall, swirly glass bottles, candy cigarettes in delicate cellophane wrappers. Often she buys them comic books—she calls them 'funny books'—such as *Porky Pig* and *Daffy Duck*, picked from a tall newsstand that squeaks when rotated. He is enchanted by their covers, by the slick, glossy paper and vivid colorizations, the pictures between filmy, rough-edged pages that he can follow, and in a sense, 'read.' But what affects him the most, what he wants most to know better, are those things he can see and touch and hear but not read—the marks laid out in tidy rows within the body of the pictures; the roll of the cash register's tumbler as his mother pays for the books; the runes ticking past on the gas pump as his father fills the tank.

"Thirty-six cents a gallon," his father always says, shaking his head.

"And 10 cents for a funny book!" says his mother.

Then, as his father turns the key and they rattle onto the road in the old Chevy work truck, Elvis takes over, singing "Suspicious Minds."

And they go *riding.*

THEY RIDE EVERYWHERE, but he can only imagine what goes on in the farmhouses and the office buildings they pass. He imagines that technicians, who work underground in cramped rooms—rooms full of control panels and television screens—operate traffic lights. That they go in and out through manholes and work down there day and night. He imagines them in gray coveralls with patches on the sleeves—three solid circles, red, yellow, and green. He imagines that *The Creature from the Black Lagoon* was filmed in Spokane's Manito Park, on a boat in Mirror Lake, across from his grandmother's house, and that manhole covers steam because the traffic technicians' rooms—like those of the submarine on *Voyage to the Bottom of the Sea*—are pressurized.

But the ride is not always wonderful. When his parents buy a Ford station wagon in 1970 the family celebrates by going to an all-you-can-eat Chinese buffet, where he gorges himself on cheese mussels, which he loves but cannot digest. He christens the new car by vomiting all over its rear storage compartment, the result of which is a carpet of cheese-mussel vomit—drying on the upholstery, and on the groceries, cracking. His mother thinks it is an isolated case of motion sickness, brought on by the excitement of the new car, and by loving cheese mussels too much. They pull over at a Phillips 66 station where she cleans it all up.

Because the wagon has a back seat he starts bringing along his Marx play-sets—Marx's Prehistoric Scenes, Marx's Modern Farm, Marx's Service Station, Marx's Cape Kennedy, all in tin cases with vinyl handles, like attachés. He opens them on his lap, unfolding new worlds—worlds filled with fences and tractors and service stations, but also cycad trees, dinosaurs, Saturn V rockets—four-color comic book worlds of cyan, magenta, yellow, and black.

One afternoon they are riding along Trent Avenue when the light of the setting sun is blocked by an enormous sheet-metal building. The building looks like an aircraft hangar and bears a massive logo high above its daylight windows—sleek yellow letters on a starry black field—like the titles at the beginning of *Star Trek*.

It is obvious to him that this is where they film the show. He supposes they have the entire ship in there, illuminated by huge lights, supported by lattices of scaffolding. For the first time he thinks of the future—not his future, not tomorrow or the next day or the day after—the future, a future colored Astronaut White, Galaxy Gold, and Re-entry Red. A future his mother and father say will be here before he knows.

I | The Sound of Trouble

HE IS SITTING at the dining room table before a long, low window, building plastic model kits with his brother, when he first hears it—a rumbling and a snarling, coming up the road, coming closer to their house. Out of the corner of his eye he sees a ghostly white blur, a car, swoop into the driveway. Its headlights dazzle his vision as it draws closer to the window. He watches their beams move across the schematics spread over the table—lighting up the *U.S.S. Enterprise's* saucer section, still attached to its mold, setting the ship's cigar-shaped secondary hull on fire, key-lighting its long, tubular warp nacelles. The beams sets the tap water to shimmer in a little porcelain bowl, where strips of red and gold decals float. They glint off the edge of an orange-white tube of Testors glue. Then they're gone.

He looks out the window, nimbuses of light still imprinted on his eyes.In their place sits the car, headlamps cooling, fading to black, plumes of exhaust rising. It is long and low and Astronaut white. Its driver's door swings open, as he has seen the hatch of the Apollo spacecraft swing open after splashdown. His father emerges, dressed in his baggy white paint clothes: his hair is greased back, his face tanned; he is wearing aviator glasses—an astronaut returned to earth.

The Kid doesn't say anything, just watches as his dad's paint truck swings into the drive behind the car. Out climbs Fast Eddy, also still in his paint clothes. He is smoking a cigarette and carrying a can of Olympia beer. "The man is 40 going on 60," his mother once described him on the phone, "but is our star employee." His father says Fast Eddy can double-coat the interior of a medium-sized home in less than a work day, all by himself.

"Hey, Eddy!" shouts his brother. He gets up and hurries out, the screen door banging behind him.

The Kid follows, gluey fingertips sticking to the schematics, causing them to swish from the table, spilling the model's pieces. There is a click as the bathroom door is unlatched. He pauses at the screen, looking over his shoulder.

His mother stands bolt upright, looking beyond him at the car. She is buttoning her blouse with one hand, holding a small mirror in the other. Her face has been tanned over the summer, her dark-blonde hair bleached gold; still she seems blanched, her expression blank. She reminds him of the astronaut in *2001: A Space Odyssey,* Bowman, after passing through the Star Gate—paralyzed, transformed. A man his mother described as having just seen it all, "the beginning, the end, *everything*."

She sets the mirror down and steadies herself against the table. Her expression softens. She doesn't quite shine, as would be typical, but something replaces the mask; something in the eyes only, something akin to her true self—something warm, blush, living.

"Go on ahead," she says. "I'll pick that up."

And she smiles—sweetly, wanly.

THE BOYS RACE out to the car amidst a September sunset—the Kid, now six, and his brother, now nine.

They circle the car in opposite directions as it idles in the pre-twilight, the brother laughing, hollering out, the Kid tentative, silent, speculative.

"S-S!" shouts the brother, "It's an S-S!"

"Sheldon Spitzer, how about that?" says Fast Eddy.

"Right," chuckles the brother. "Try Super Sport."

The Kid completes his circuit, stares at the black-accented grill and the chromed 'S-S' indicia centered there. He can't yet read but recognizes the shapes. S-S. As in U.S.S. As in not just car. As in *Enterprise.*

His father opens the passenger's side door, gestures to him like Bob Barker on *The Price is Right.* "…a brand-new car!"

A big teenager who lives next door lopes across the field, arms swinging. "Just about," he drawls. Everyone calls him B.B.—because his name is 'Billy,' and because he walks like Bigfoot. "1968—five years old. Nice El Camino."

"El Camino," repeats the Kid. He steps close and stares in at the cab: at the chromed shifter and radio and the futuristic speedometer and council clock; at the single black bench seat and the flesh-colored carpeting—which rises, in the middle of the floor, to meet the shifter's rubber baffling. He hardly notices his brother opening the driver's door and slipping behind the wheel. He hardly notices anything but the carpeted floor and the sumptuous mound, which together form a hammock, almost, beneath the dashboard's black, enveloping shelter.

"Where the heck is everyone going to sit?" says his brother, rocking the wheel, pretending to drive. The dome light causes a queer play of shadows over his face, teasing out features the Kid, the very mirror of their father, does not possess.

"Oh, I'll just ride in the back," drawls B.B.

"There's plenty of room for everyone," says his father. "You're not that big yet."

“I will be,” says the brother. He pulls a handle under the dash, pops the hood.

The Kid doesn’t say anything, only peers through the rear window at the payload bay, which takes the place of back seats.

His father has purchased a white 1968 El Camino with a black vinyl roof and matching decals, but he sees a spaceship, an aerodynamic domicile: a rocket with twin-domed hood scoops and louvered ports and long, pin-striped rear quarter panels, like warp nacelles, which through an alchemy known to Federation engineers and certain boys and girls can fold space, can warp time.

They huddle around the engine compartment—Fast Eddy, father, Sheldon and B.B.—as he peers between, glimpses something black and chrome and complicated before his brother blocks the view—purposely, it seems. He keeps trying to see as Fast Eddy talks like he paints, fast.

“It’s not the cylinders themselves that move, see. It’s the pistons.

Each cylinder has a spark plug, which causes compressed gas to combust and re-combust—bang-bang-bang, like that. The sparks are timed so that they push the pistons down and drive the crankshaft…”

“How many cylinders?” asks the brother.

“Eight,” says his father.

“Hah!” cries B.B. “Explains that!”

“Explains what?”

“The sound of trouble when you pulled in,” says B.B.

The Kid is on the pavement, crawling between their legs. He figures if he can’t see it from above he’ll see it from below.

Fast Eddy says: “Huh? No, that’s not the sound of trouble.

That's glass packs. The sound of trouble is when something goes *wrong.*"

The Kid is on his back now. He is reaching up into the purring, whirring compartment, intending to pull himself farther under, when his father grabs him by both ankles, yanks him out.

"Aye, aye, aye!" he shouts. He pulls him to his feet, draws him away from the others. "You don't ever reach into machinery like that. Not ever, Buddy!"

He looks at his father numbly, feeling foolish beyond words. He knows that Sheldon and Fast Eddy and B.B. are looking at him also, but does not return their gaze.

His father massages his shoulders and points him toward the field, to where his Styrachosaurus model sits like an ornament on the old Ford wagon. "Someone's going to make off with that," he says.

He focuses on it, squinting in the setting sun. His father gives him a nudge. He runs after his model.

GRASSHOPPERS SCATTER, ticking and whirring, as he moves through the field. He picks the model up off the hood of the wagon—one of its legs falls off, tumbling into the grass, which is knee-high, golden. He picks it up and examines it. The breeze tosses his hair. He looks past the green, pebble-textured model part—at the old Ford station wagon. Although he rode in it only yesterday, the light- brown car looks as though it has been here forever, merged with the grass and weeds—as though it were already receding from him, from the family. He looks at the new car, at his father and brother and B.B. and Fast Eddy. He opens the driver's door of the wagon, watching them, and sits in the doorframe.

He tries to fit the Styrachosaur's leg back onto its body, but discovers that the little plastic knob that holds it in place is broken.

The breeze blows and ruffles the grass. He looks at their new house, which is painted white with black accents, like his father's new car—thinks of his mother holding her hand-mirror. He does not know why he should think of this just now, or why the thought should bother him. His earlier notion of folding space and warping time seems suddenly threatening. There is something beneath the idea, something he can divine but not apprehend, a hidden layer.

His brother shouts, "Can I rev it? Can I rev it just once?"

"Hold on, Buddy," says their father. "Mary Lee! Let's go for a ride!"

The Kid fidgets. He waits for her to come out, feeling suddenly queasy, feeling as though she might in fact not come out—the fear is so alien that it seems to rise up in him like bile.

She emerges at last, wearing her fuzzy coat and carrying coats for his brother and himself: new coats, fresh as the paint on the new car, and the new house, and his father's job-sites—all the schools and grocery stores across Spokane his parents have bid on and won. "The boys have school tomorrow," she says, adding, "Where's the Kid?"

She looks around for him, spies him through the weeds. "What are you doing out there? Come join the party."

He wonders why he can't stop shaking. Why his stomach bucks and twists; why he's convinced the earth might suddenly fall away, the sun and moon blink out, the clouds roil black.

"Okay! Give her a rev!" shouts his father. The car's engine revs and roars.

The Kid leaps to his feet, startled. Something happens—it seems to him the universe itself just ignites and rolls over, right there, under his shoes. He falls down instantly, quaking and dry-heaving.

The car's engine roars and roars. "That's enough!" barks his father. Fast Eddy laughs.

The Kid coughs and spits and wipes his mouth. He is shaking uncontrollably. He peers through the grass and weeds, sees his mother hurrying toward him, her tanned face and blonde hair appearing gray in the waning sunlight. He gets up suddenly and runs toward her, his own blonde hair flying.

She has hardly finished stooping when he collides against her breast.

"I—I was afraid—Bowman—how you said—I don't—I don't want..." He bursts into tears, presses into her coat.

She rocks him back and forth, patting his back. "There, there, Sweetie. Now, now."

He doesn't know what to say—what it is that he truly even feels. Something has brushed him, has bruised him.

"Something awful," he says.

"Shhh," she says. "There is nothing awful." She runs her hands over his hair, kisses his forehead. They remain that way for several minutes, saying nothing. At last she turns him away gently. "There's only that, see?"

She points to the setting sun, to the clouds shot through with red and gold.

He stares at them, sniffling. Suddenly everything seems perfect again—safe, spacious, mild. The air is cool, and fragrant with his mother's hairspray. He senses that she alone is interested in him; not his father, certainly not his brother—not his Sunday school teachers or the girls across the street. After awhile he says, "What if it goes out? What if—God turns it off?"

She plucks at his hair, straightens it out. "He turns it off every night. And what happens every morning?"

He swipes at his eyes, sniffs.

She retakes his shoulders gently in her hands, turns him back to face her. “What happens every morning?”

“He turns it back on again.”

She smiles. “Which means it never really went out.”

He stares at her as she releases his shoulders—slowly, delicately, as though she was balancing him on a wire. “My favorite Martian,” she says. She tries to smooth his cowlicks, “Sensitive antennae and all.” She laughs. “I don’t know how we’ll get through sometimes.”

The Kid smiles, a bit awkwardly, then turns to look at the sun—sees the station wagon silhouetted against it. “It looks lonely out there,” he says.

“It’s just a car, Sweetie. It can’t feel lonely.” She places a hand on his shoulder, steering him away. “Besides, we have a new one now.”

www.ingramcontent.com/pod-product-compliance
Lightning Source LLC
Chambersburg PA
CBHW061101100726
47911CB00012B/339
* 9 7 8 1 7 3 2 1 4 0 1 3 4 *